Apple Core

Friendship Square

Cornucopia

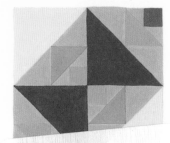

Harvest Home

Tea Leaves

# The Quilter's Kitchen

AN ELM CREEK QUILTS NOVEL WITH RECIPES

## Jennifer Chiaverini

Simon & Schuster
New York  London  Toronto  Sydney

Simon & Schuster
1230 Avenue of the Americas
New York, NY 10020

First Simon & Schuster hardcover edition October 2008

SIMON & SCHUSTER and colophon are
registered trademarks of Simon & Schuster, Inc.

For information about special discounts for bulk purchases,
please contact Simon & Schuster Special Sales at
1-800-456-6798 or business@simonandschuster.com

Endpaper designs by Melanie Marder Parks
Designed by Davina Mock-Maniscalco

Manufactured in the United States of America

1   3   5   7   9   10   8   6   4   2

Library of Congress Cataloging-in-Publication Data
Chiaverini, Jennifer.
The quilter's kitchen : an Elm Creek Quilts novel with recipes / Jennifer Chiaverini.
p.   cm.
1. Compson, Sylvia (Fictitious character)—Fiction.   2. Quiltmakers—
Fiction.   3. Women cooks—Fiction.   4. Food writing—Fiction.   5. Cookery—
Fiction.   6. Quilting—Fiction.   7. Quilts—Fiction.   8. Pennsylvania—
Fiction.   9. Domestic fiction.   I. Title.
PS3553.H473Q575   2008
813'.54—dc22                         2008016554

ISBN-13: 978-1-4165-8329-5
ISBN-10:     1-4165-8329-7

For my aunt,
Becki Riechman,
who seasons every family gathering
with laughter, warmth, and love

# Contents

# CHAPTER ONE

# Welcome Banquet

 As Jeremy turned the car off the main highway from Waterford and onto the narrow gravel road that wound through the leafy wood encircling the Bergstrom estate, Anna instinctively clutched her seat cushion with one hand and braced herself against the dashboard with the other. "Maybe when we're finished remodeling the kitchen," she said, voice shaking with each bump and jolt, "we can convince Sylvia to do something about this road."

Jeremy kept his eyes on the winding way that led into the forest; if a car approached from the opposite direction, he would have to react quickly and pull halfway off the road to avoid a collision. Both sides of his car were already marked with fine scratches from past diversions into the underbrush. "I doubt it," he replied, his wire-rimmed glasses sliding down his nose a millimeter or two with every pothole. "Sylvia's a traditionalist. The longer you know her, the more you'll realize that she's reluctant to alter the old family estate too much."

"She's letting me make big changes to the kitchen," Anna reminded him.

Jeremy shrugged and offered her his familiar cheerful, crooked grin. "Only because she didn't think you'd take the job otherwise."

As much as Anna was thrilled with her new position as Elm Creek Manor's chef, she had to admit that Sylvia had guessed correctly. She would never forget her first glimpse of the kitchen when she had come to the manor for her job interview. It was larger than she expected to find in a building constructed in 1858, but there was not a single appliance post-1945 except for a tiny microwave on the counter, possibly the first ever invented by the look of it. The pantry was spacious and well stocked, but poorly lit and so badly organized that it would have taken Anna longer to find ingredients for one of her signature dishes than to mix them together. And as for the cooking utensils left to soak in the sink . . . The whisk looked to be at least fifty years old, which wouldn't have bothered her had it not been bent out of shape, and the hand mixer had rust, actual rust, on the handle. How the Elm Creek Quilters had managed to feed fifty-plus people three meals a day with that four-burner gas stove was a mystery, but Anna knew that she couldn't work in such conditions, not after being spoiled by the sparkling clean, modern facilities at Waterford College. Fortunately Sylvia had agreed that the kitchen was long overdue for an upgrade, and she had accepted Anna's condition for taking the job.

Now that Elm Creek Quilt Camp had ended for the season, Sylvia and Anna would launch the remodeling process in earnest. With weeks of planning and hours of consultation behind them, in two days they would usher in a team of workmen to tear out old cupboards and haul away dilapidated appliances, to demolish the wall between the kitchen and the west sitting room, to install new wiring, lighting, shelving, appliances, and everything else Anna desired and Sylvia's budget would allow. If all went well, Anna would have a fully operational, professional kitchen in time for the holiday feasts she intended to prepare for her new colleagues.

She hoped, in time, that they would become her friends.

Late-morning sunlight broke through the leafy wood, gold and rust and scarlet with autumn, as the road forked, wound through the trees, and emerged beside a sunlit apple orchard. They passed a red barn, climbed a low hill, and crossed the bridge over Elm Creek. All at once the manor came into view—three stories of gray stone and dark wood surrounded by autumnal beauty.

Anna knew the Elm Creek Quilters considered the grand

manor a second home. She was an Elm Creek Quilter now, too, she reminded herself. Perhaps in time Elm Creek Manor would become as important to her as it was to her new coworkers.

On the other side of the creek, the road broadened into a parking lot that circled two towering elms. "Call me when you want me to pick you up," Jeremy offered as he parked near the foot of the back stairs.

"I can take the bus," Anna said. She couldn't help feeling as if she were imposing on his generosity. It was one thing for him to drive her to work when his girlfriend, Summer, had lived at the manor, but now that Summer was attending graduate school in Chicago, Jeremy had no reason to come so far out of his way. Anna and Jeremy were friends and neighbors, with apartments on opposite sides of the hall in a building not far from the Waterford College campus, but these almost daily drives were a lot to ask even of a friend. But every time Anna mentioned the bus, Jeremy shook his head and drove her anyway. Anna suspected that Summer had asked him to bring her since she was new, to help her feel less like an outsider. Or maybe the Elm Creek Quilters were afraid that she would grow tired of the long walk from the bus stop, and they had enlisted Jeremy's help to make sure she didn't wear out her shoes. Or maybe Jeremy was just a nice guy and she was taking advantage of him.

Whatever the reason, and despite the occasional pang of guilt, secretly Anna was glad that their carpooling had not ended with Summer's departure. The bus's circuitous route would have added two hours to her daily commute, and she would have missed Jeremy's company.

"I'll have my cell on," Jeremy said, as if she had not mentioned the bus this time, either. Surely Summer had asked him to babysit her. That had to be it.

Anna returned Jeremy's grin, waved good-bye, and climbed the four stone steps to the back door of Elm Creek Manor. The kitchen was through the first doorway on the left, and from within came the sound of someone clattering pots and pans and what sounded like cookie sheets.

Anna hung her jacket in the hall closet and entered the kitchen, which already seemed strangely bare with the long wooden table and the benches that usually flanked it missing. Clad in a burgundy cardigan and black slacks, her silver-gray hair held back in a tortoise-shell comb, Sylvia Bergstrom Compson, Master Quilter and founder of Elm Creek Quilts, sat cross-legged on the floor, transferring skillets and saucepans into a carton. She glanced up and smiled, feathery lines etched around her eyes and mouth deepening, but the fondness in her expression did not lessen her air of command, as if she were a woman who was accustomed to voicing her opinions and having others carefully listen.

"Matt and Andrew moved the table and benches into the dining room, out of the way," Sylvia said, answering Anna's unspoken question. Brushing dust from her hands, she rose, far more slender than Anna and nearly as tall, with only the slightest stoop to her shoulders. A pair of glasses hung around her neck on a silver chain. "I haven't decided what to do with them yet. They'll seem out of place in our new kitchen, and yet they've been in the family so long I can't bear to get rid of them."

"I'm sure we can find a place for them somewhere," said Anna. "We don't have to get rid of everything, not if it's useful or has sentimental value."

"You're thinking just like my Bergstrom ancestors," said Sylvia dryly. "Remind me to show you the attic someday. No, we can't keep everything. That's the whole point of our work today, isn't it, to clear out the old and make way for the new?"

Anna hesitated. "I thought we were just going to pack up the dishes and cookware and move everything out of the way before the contractor demolishes the cabinets. I assumed we'd put everything back afterward."

"And spoil your lovely new kitchen with rusty old pots and pans?" Sylvia shook her head. "Out of the question."

"Sometimes old pots cook better than new," said Anna, thinking of the cast-iron cookware she had long admired. She was itching to cook up a ratatouille in the Dutch oven that had belonged to Sylvia's great-aunt. "Let's not discard things arbitrarily just because they clash with the paint and granite."

Sylvia smiled, amused by Anna's reference to their many contentious debates with their contractor's designer, who held strong opinions about the merits of particular color combinations. "Agreed. If I want to toss something out but you want to keep it, I'll let you have the last word. This kitchen will be your workspace, after all."

"But it's more than that," Anna said. "A kitchen is the heart of a home. Think of how much time the Elm Creek Quilters spend in this room, discussing quilt patterns and lesson plans over coffee and cake. Your guests, too. In the few weeks I've been here, I've noticed that time and time again, quilt campers find their way to the kitchen."

"They follow their noses," Sylvia said. "More so than ever since you came on board."

"It's also the first room campers pass when they come through the back door," Anna added, "and except for registration morning, that's the door they use most frequently."

Sylvia nodded, thoughtful. "It never occurred to me, but perhaps the kitchen is just as important as the front foyer is for offering our guests a warm welcome to the manor."

In Anna's opinion, the kitchen played that role in every home. "We could always move the registration tables in here," she joked as she knelt beside a lower cabinet. Inside she found cake pans of all shapes and sizes, definitely worth keeping. She pulled over an empty carton and carefully stacked the pans within it.

"Even after we knock out the wall and expand into the sitting room, we won't have enough space for that," said Sylvia. "Our campers will have to wait until the Welcome Banquet to get an official greeting from your kitchen."

The Welcome Banquet: the eagerly anticipated commencement of each new week of camp. The banquet hall, transformed by white linen tablecloths, crystal, and candlelight, set the proper festive tone for the days ahead, a week devoted to learning, sharing, and enjoying a respite from the cares of ordinary life. Anna had prepared the delicious feast for the last few weeks of the camp season, and she had been delighted by the campers' rave reviews—not to mention those of the Elm Creek Quilters. She was pleased to know that she played such an important role in creating a celebratory mood and a sense of anticipation for the week ahead.

But many quilt campers found their way to the kitchen before they sat down to supper in the banquet hall.

"The kitchen has to be a welcoming place for our campers," Anna mused, sitting back on her heels and forgetting the bakeware for a moment.

"It will be," Sylvia promised. "The new seating will give

campers a place to relax with a cup of coffee or a snack, or if they just want a cozy place to chat with friends. You might find yourself entertaining an audience while you prepare meals. I hope you won't mind."

"Not at all. It would be fun, like having my own cooking show." Anna drew her long, dark brown French braid over her shoulder, tucked a few loose strands back into the plait, and tightened the band on the end. "But that makes it even more important to create an inviting atmosphere, don't you think? Cozy seats, coffee, and snacks aren't enough. We need to find a way to make this kitchen serve up the spirit of Elm Creek Quilts just as it serves delicious meals. Somehow—and I don't know how yet—we have to give our guests a sense of the history of the manor as well as its exciting present. I want to honor the traditions of the Bergstrom family as well as all the people, Elm Creek Quilters and campers alike, who make Elm Creek Quilt Camp such a unique place. I want to bring all those flavors together, right here in this room."

Sylvia regarded Anna over the rims of her glasses for a moment. When a smile quirked in the corners of Sylvia's mouth, Anna knew her new employer was pleased with her ideas, but also amused that she hoped for so much from a simple kitchen. "That's a tall order," said Sylvia, brushing crumbs from a dented muffin tin.

"I've trained in some of the finest kitchens in Pennsylvania, under some of the most demanding chefs you'd ever meet," Anna replied. "I know how to fill a tall order."

Sylvia smiled. "Spoken like a true Elm Creek Quilter."

Anna fervently hoped so. She didn't feel like one, not quite yet, and she wanted to, more than anything.

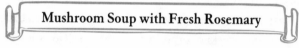

### Mushroom Soup with Fresh Rosemary

Yield: about 16 cups

1 tablespoon unsalted butter

1 Spanish onion, halved and coarsely chopped or sliced

2½ to 3 pounds button mushrooms, wiped clean and coarsely chopped, stems included

2 teaspoons dried rosemary

2 Idaho potatoes, unpeeled, diced (about 2 cups)

12 cups low-sodium chicken broth

2 tablespoons dry sherry

1 cup light cream

Kosher salt and black pepper

Fresh rosemary leaves, for garnish

Place a large heavy-bottomed soup pot over medium heat and when it is hot, add the butter. When the butter has melted, add the onion, and cook until tender, about 10 minutes.

Add the mushrooms and rosemary and cook until the mushrooms release their juices, about 15 minutes. Then add the potatoes, chicken broth, and sherry, raise the heat to high and bring to a boil. Reduce the heat to low and cook until the potatoes are tender, about 20 minutes.

Remove the solids and place in a blender or food processor fitted with a steel blade. Process, in batches, until completely smooth, gradually adding the remaining broth and cream. Season with salt and black pepper. Serve garnished with fresh rosemary.

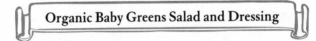

## Organic Baby Greens Salad and Dressing

Yield: dressing for 8 to 12 cups organic baby greens

For the dressing:

1 garlic clove, chopped
½ teaspoon Dijon mustard
2 tablespoons balsamic vinegar

¼ teaspoon kosher salt
⅛ teaspoon black pepper
¼ cup extra-virgin olive oil

For the salad:

8–12 cups organic baby greens
1 bunch radishes, trimmed and thinly sliced

*To make the dressing*: Place the garlic, mustard, vinegar, salt, and pepper in a blender and process until thoroughly combined. While the machine is running, gradually add the olive oil. Transfer to a glass container, cover and refrigerate up to 1 month. If the oil separates from the vinegar, shake it vigorously. If it solidifies, leave it out at room temperature for a few minutes and then shake well.

*To make the salad:* put the baby greens and radish slices in a large salad bowl, add the dressing, and gently mix. Serve immediately.

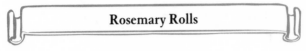

## Rosemary Rolls

Yield: 12 large rolls

3 cups all-purpose flour

1 tablespoon baking powder

1 teaspoon kosher salt

1 teaspoon baking soda

1 teaspoon finely chopped fresh rosemary

12 tablespoons (1½ sticks) unsalted butter, chilled or frozen, cut into thin slices

1 cup sour cream, or full-fat or low-fat yogurt

Preheat the oven to 425 degrees F. Line a baking sheet with parchment paper.

Place the flour, baking powder, salt, baking soda, and rosemary in the bowl of a food processor fitted with a steel blade and mix to combine. While the processor is going, add the butter a few slices at a time, and process until the mixture resembles cornmeal. Transfer it to a large mixing bowl; add the sour cream and, using a wooden spoon, mix until combined. Divide the mixture into 12 pieces and place them on the prepared baking sheet. Transfer to the oven and bake until golden brown, 12 to 15 minutes.

## Roast Chicken with Cilantro and Orange

Serves 6 to 8

1 bunch cilantro, leaves chopped, stems discarded

3 garlic cloves

2 shallots, halved

2 teaspoons kosher salt

1 teaspoon black pepper

1 teaspoon crushed red pepper flakes (optional)

Zest and juice of 1 orange

⅓ cup olive oil

Two 3-pound chickens, necks and giblets removed

1 orange, quartered

Place the cilantro, garlic, shallots, salt, pepper, and crushed red pepper flakes, if using, in the bowl of a food processor fitted with a steel blade and pulse until everything is chopped. Add the orange zest and juice and pulse again. While the processor is running, slowly add the olive oil.

Rinse the chickens in cold water until the water runs clear. Place each chicken in a large resealable plastic bag and add half the marinade. Be sure the cilantro-orange mixture gets into all the cavities. Refrigerate at least 2 hours and up to over-night. Turn the bag occasionally.

Preheat the oven to 350 degrees F.

Place the chickens on a roasting pan and put 2 orange quarters in the cavity of each chicken.

Transfer to the oven and roast until the juices run clear, about 1 hour 15 minutes. Let rest 10 minutes and serve.

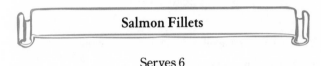

## Salmon Fillets

Serves 6

2 tablespoons Dijon mustard

2 tablespoons light brown sugar

1½ to 2 pounds salmon fillets (tiny bones removed with a
    tweezer), cut in half

½ teaspoon kosher salt

¼ teaspoon black pepper

Preheat the broiler.

Place the mustard and brown sugar in a small bowl and mix to combine.

Place the salmon fillets in a large flameproof baking dish

and smother with the mustard mixture. Sprinkle with the salt and pepper and place under the broiler. Cook until browned on top and just undercooked inside, 5 to 6 minutes.

Cut each half into 3 pieces and serve immediately.

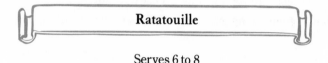

### Ratatouille

Serves 6 to 8

2 tablespoons olive oil

1 Spanish or red onion, chopped

4 garlic cloves, minced

1 medium eggplant, peeled and diced

4 small or 2 large zucchini, diced

1 red bell pepper, diced

2 cups diced tomatoes, canned (with liquid) or fresh

1 lemon, quartered

Shaved or grated Parmesan cheese

Fresh basil leaves

Place a medium-size stockpot over medium-low heat and when it is hot, add the oil. Add the onion and garlic and cook 10 minutes. Add the eggplant and zucchini, cover and cook 10 minutes. Add the red bell pepper and cook, covered, for 10 minutes.

Add the tomatoes and cook, uncovered, for 10 minutes if they are canned, and for 20 minutes if fresh.

Cover and refrigerate overnight in a storage container, or serve immediately, garnished with the lemon quarters, Parmesan cheese, and basil.

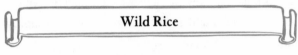

## Wild Rice

Yield: about 6 cups

⅔ cup wild rice

⅓ cup brown jasmine rice

2⅔ cups water

2 tablespoons unsalted butter

1 Spanish onion, chopped

1 carrot, finely chopped

1 celery stalk, finely chopped

2 teaspoons dried thyme

1 cup dried cranberries or currants

1 cup lightly toasted, coarsely chopped pecans,
        walnuts, or hazelnuts

¼ cup fresh parsley leaves, finely chopped

½ teaspoon kosher salt

¼ teaspoon black pepper

Place the rices and water in a large pot and bring to a boil over high heat. Reduce the heat to low, cover, and cook until tender, about 45 minutes. Drain, if necessary.

Place a large skillet over medium heat and when it is hot, add the butter. Add the onion, carrot, celery, and thyme and cook until translucent, about 8 to 10 minutes. Set aside until the rice is finished. Add the rice, dried cranberries, nuts, parsley, salt, and pepper and gently stir until heated through, about 3 minutes. Serve immediately.

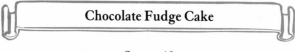

### Chocolate Fudge Cake

Serves 12

1 pound semisweet chocolate, chopped
1½ cups (3 sticks) unsalted butter, chopped
8 large eggs, at room temperature
1 cup sugar
1 tablespoon vanilla extract
1 tablespoon confectioners' sugar

Preheat the oven to 350 degrees F. Grease the sides and bottom of a 9-inch springform pan and wrap with heavy-duty aluminum foil.

Place the chocolate and butter in a large bowl set over a pot of gently simmering water. Stir to combine.

Place the eggs, sugar, and vanilla extract in the bowl of a stand mixer fitted with a whisk and process until just combined, about 30 seconds. Add the melted chocolate and mix until just combined. Pour the mixture into the prepared pan. Set in a larger roasting pan and fill the roasting pan with hot water halfway up the sides of the springform pan.

Transfer to the oven and bake until the cake is set, about 1 hour. Cool 10 minutes in the pan, then run a knife along the sides and gently unmold. Set aside to cool completely. Sprinkle with confectioners' sugar just before serving.

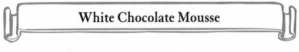

## White Chocolate Mousse

Serves 8 to 10

12 ounces white chocolate, chopped
2½ cups heavy cream
1 tablespoon Chambord or other fruit-flavored
    liqueur

Place the chocolate and 1 cup cream in a metal bowl set over a pot of gently simmering water. Stir occasionally until the chocolate is melted and the mixture is smooth. Set aside until slightly thickened and cool to the touch, 20 to 30 minutes.

Place the remaining 1½ cups cream and the liqueur in the bowl of a stand mixer fitted with a whisk and mix on high speed until the cream forms stiff peaks, about 30 seconds. Add half the whipped cream to the chocolate mixture and fold together gently; add remaining cream mixture and fold together until no streaks remain. Transfer it to a serving bowl and refrigerate until set, about 1 hour.

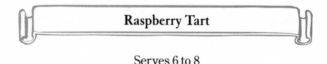

### Raspberry Tart

Serves 6 to 8

For the crust:

¾ cup plus 1 tablespoon all-purpose flour

3 tablespoons sugar

¼ teaspoon kosher salt

6 tablespoons unsalted butter, frozen and cut into pieces

1 to 2 tablespoons cold water

For the filling:

4 ounces cream cheese, at room temperature

½ cup low-fat Greek yogurt

1 teaspoon vanilla extract

¼ cup superfine sugar

1 tablespoon honey


4 to 5 cups fresh raspberries (or other berries)


Preheat the oven to 350 degrees F.

*To make the crust:* Place the flour, sugar, and salt in a food processor fitted with a steel blade and pulse to mix. While the processor is going, add the butter, 1 piece at a time; and pulse until the mixture resembles cornmeal. Add the water and pulse until the mixture is still coarse but just comes together into a ball. Press down into an 11-inch round tart pan (with a removable bottom). Transfer the pan to the oven and bake until just starting to color, about 25 minutes. Do not overcook or the crust will be too hard. Set aside to cool completely.

*To make the filling:* Place the cream cheese and yogurt in a small bowl and mash until the mixture is smooth. Mix in the remaining ingredients and set aside.

Spread the filling in the cooled tart shell and then top with the berries. Serve immediately or cover and refrigerate up to 4 hours.

You can make the shell and filling 1 day ahead and assemble it just prior to serving.

## Champagne Cocktail

Serves 8

8 sugar cubes
Angostura bitters
One 750 ml bottle Champagne, chilled
8 strips lemon peel (1 lemon)

Place a sugar cube in each of 8 champagne glasses. Sprinkle with a few drops of Angostura and then fill the glass with Champagne. Twist the peels and drop into the Champagne. Serve immediately.

# CHAPTER TWO

# Quilting Bee

 Anna emptied one cabinet and moved on to the next, where she discovered a cache of pans in such poor condition that no amount of scrubbing could restore them. Apparently Sylvia had not exaggerated when she explained that her Bergstrom ancestors never threw anything away. "I think that if I soak this skillet and go at it with a steel wool pad, I'll scrub a hole right through it before I get to the bottom of the rust," Anna said, tossing it into the box she and Sylvia had designated for junk.

"I suspect you'll see many more pots and pans in even worse condition than that before we're through." Sylvia eyed the remaining cabinets ruefully. "If you knew as well as I do what awaits us behind those doors and within those drawers, you'd realize how formidable this job is going to be. Perhaps we should have allowed for more than two days to finish the job, or enlisted more help, if I could have tricked the other Elm Creek Quilters into it."

"I noticed that the manor is unusually quiet today," said Anna, smiling. "I guess your friends conveniently found themselves with more important things to do—and well out of shouting distance from the kitchen."

"Oh, the manor's no quieter than any other weekend when camp isn't in session." Sylvia nudged a half-full carton out of the way with her foot so she could open a new cabinet. "You've been here only when we've had a houseful of guests—footfalls overhead, laughter in the halls, sewing machines abuzz. On Sunday mornings in the summer, I find the few quiet hours between camp sessions restful, but I confess I miss the bustle and excitement once autumn sets in, and quiet becomes the norm."

"There's a big difference between a few quiet hours before the campers arrive on registration day and weeks of silence with the manor mostly empty."

"There is, indeed. And yet it isn't that quiet. I have my husband Andrew for company, of course, as well as Sarah and Matt McClure, and Gretchen and Joe Hartley. But two Elm Creek Quilters and their husbands make only a fraction of the noise of a houseful of quilt campers."

"Just wait until Sarah has her twins," said Anna. "You'll

look back on the busiest days of quilt camp and remember them as quiet and peaceful!"

Sylvia laughed. "I'm looking forward to it. I could use a little more noise around here. But don't misinterpret the lack of activity around here this morning as abandonment by our friends. If I had thought to ask them to join us, I'm sure they would have willingly agreed to help."

Anna's heart warmed at Sylvia's choice of words: *our* friends. "I'm sure they would have. I was only teasing. Quilters are some of the most helpful people you'll ever meet."

"I should have organized a bee," Sylvia mused, frowning at a cracked ceramic casserole before dumping it into the junk carton. "Many hands make light work, or so the saying goes. If quilters can come together for a quilting bee, why not to clear out a kitchen?"

"I've never been to a quilting bee," Anna admitted, "unless you count the ones my aunt used to hold at her quilt shop. Sometimes when a favorite customer had a large quilt to layer and baste, my aunt would invite her to push a few tables together and spread out the backing, batting, and top at the back of the store. Often other customers would join in to help. My aunt also organized a regular monthly meeting to make quilts for charity—tiny quilts for the preemie ward at the local hospital, children's cuddle quilts for firefighters and police to give to families they served, and fund-raising quilts for just about every worthy cause you could imagine. My aunt often told me that she believed businesses ought to give back to the communities that kept them in business."

Sylvia nodded approvingly. "We Elm Creek Quilters ought to do more of that. Often we become so caught up in the demands of running quilt camp that we forget to be charitable. Oh, we think about it, but then we have registration forms to process and class samples to stitch and so many other duties that I'm afraid good works slip to the bottom of our to-do lists."

"What about during the off-season?" said Anna. "Without campers to look after, I'm sure we could find time to work on a project for a good cause here in the Elm Creek Valley. We could invite the Waterford Quilting Guild to join us."

"An excellent idea," Sylvia declared. "After all, quilting bees aren't only about getting the work done. An honest quilter will admit that socializing is just as important as sewing, and always has been, ever since our pioneer ancestors invented the bee. My great-great-aunt Gerda wrote about a local nineteenth-century quilting bee tradition in her memoir."

In Gerda's day, Sylvia explained, daughters would learn to sew by piecing quilts, and a worthy young woman was expected to complete twelve quilt tops by the time she reached marriageable age. The thirteenth quilt was to be her masterpiece, as fine a quilt as she could make, putting the best of her needlework talents on display as evidence that she had learned all the sewing skills she would need as a wife and mother. When the young woman became engaged, all the bride-to-be's female friends and family would gather for a quilting bee, where the thirteen pieced and appliquéd tops would be quilted and finished.

"According to Gerda's memoir," Sylvia added, "the men attended, too, but for the food and festivities rather than the quilting."

"You can't have a gathering of quilters without food," Anna said cheerfully. "The men wouldn't want to miss out on that, even if they weren't willing and able to help the bride finish her quilts."

"Contemporary quilting bees are no different," said Sylvia. "Quilters come for the companionship, the laughter, the sharing of confidences—and to swap patterns and recipes with friends and neighbors."

Anna resolved that whenever the Elm Creek Quilters launched their own quilting bees, their guests would find the refreshments as well as the needlework equal to any quilting bee the Elm Creek Valley had ever seen.

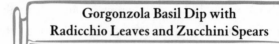

## Gorgonzola Basil Dip with
## Radicchio Leaves and Zucchini Spears

Yield: about 1½ cups

1 cup (about 11 ounces) Gorgonzola cheese,
    at room temperature
¼ cup cream cheese (regular, not whipped),
    at room temperature
⅓ cup light cream, whole milk, or buttermilk
2 teaspoons fresh lemon juice
¼ teaspoon black pepper
⅓ cup fresh basil leaves, finely chopped
¼ cup chopped lightly toasted walnuts or pine nuts
Finely chopped fresh basil leaves,
    for garnish (optional)

1 head radicchio leaves, for garnish
2 zucchini, cut into spears, for garnish

Place the cheeses and light cream in a mixing bowl and combine with a fork. Add the lemon juice and pepper and mix again.
Add the basil and nuts and add very gently (if you overmix, it
will be totally blue). Set aside, covered, for 1 hour or refriger-

ate overnight. Allow to return to room temperature before serving.

Serve garnished with the additional basil surrounded by radicchio leaves and zucchini spears.

## Thai Chicken Peanut Satay

Serves 8 to 10

For the marinade:

⅓ cup low-sodium soy sauce

¼ cup seasoned rice wine vinegar

3 tablespoons canola oil

2 tablespoons peanut oil

1 tablespoon curry powder

1 tablespoon minced gingerroot

½ teaspoon salt

½ teaspoon cayenne pepper (optional)

3 pounds skinless, boneless chicken tenders,
    trimmed of fat and pounded

For the peanut sauce:

¾ cup good quality peanut butter (no sugar)

1 cup boiling water

2 tablespoons low-sodium soy sauce

2 garlic cloves, peeled

2 teaspoons fresh lime juice

2 teaspoons light brown sugar

1 teaspoon minced fresh gingerroot

¼ teaspoon kosher salt

⅛ to ¼ teaspoon cayenne pepper


Chopped peanuts, for garnish

Chopped fresh basil leaves, for garnish

Chopped scallion greens, for garnish


*To make the marinade:* Place the soy sauce, rice wine vinegar, oils, curry powder, gingerroot, salt, and cayenne if using, in a nonreactive 3- to 4-quart bowl and mix until all the ingredients are well combined.

Add the chicken to the bowl and mix until it is completely immersed in the marinade. Cover and refrigerate at least 1 hour and up to 3 hours.

*To make the peanut sauce:* While the chicken is marinating, place the peanut butter and the boiling water in a food processor fitted with a steel blade and process until the two ingredients come together. Gradually, while the processor is running, add the remaining peanut sauce ingredients and process until creamy. Transfer to a container and refrigerate at least 1 hour and up to 1 week.

Prepare the grill or preheat the broiler. Have ready 12 wooden or metal skewers.

To cook, remove as much marinade as possible from the chicken, thread the chicken on skewers, place the kabobs on a grill, and cook until the chicken is deeply browned on the outside and no longer pink on the inside, 4 to 5 minutes on each side. Transfer to a serving platter and serve immediately garnished with the chopped peanuts, fresh basil, and scallion greens, with the peanut sauce on top or on the side.

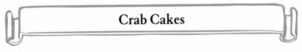

## Crab Cakes

Serves 8 as an appetizer

12 ounces crabmeat, picked over and very coarsely shredded

½ cup panko bread crumbs

¼ cup mayonnaise or whole-milk yogurt

2 tablespoons chopped fresh Italian flat-leaf parsley
    or fresh basil

1 tablespoon chopped fresh chives or scallion greens

¼ cup all-purpose flour

1 teaspoon kosher salt

2 tablespoons olive oil

1 lime or lemon, quartered

Place the crabmeat, panko, mayonnaise, parsley, and chives in a medium-size bowl and very gently combine. Form into 8 small patties. Cover and refrigerate at least 1 hour and up to 4 hours.

Place the flour and salt on a large plate. Dredge each patty in the mixture. Place a large skillet over medium-high heat and when it is hot, add the oil. Add the patties and cook until lightly browned, about 4 minutes on each side, in two batches, if necessary. Serve immediately with the lime or lemon quarters.

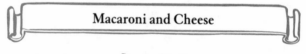

### Macaroni and Cheese

Serves 6 to 8

1 pound macaroni, elbow or other bite-size shape

4 tablespoons (½ stick) unsalted butter

¼ cup all-purpose flour

½ teaspoon kosher salt

⅛ to ¼ teaspoon white pepper

3 cups whole milk

4 cups grated cheddar cheese

1 cup grated Gruyère cheese

For the topping:

¼ cup Parmesan or Romano cheese

¼ cup finely grated cheddar cheese

2 cups Panko bread crumbs

2 tablespoons melted unsalted butter

Bring a large pot of water to a boil over high heat. Add the pasta and cook until al dente. Drain and transfer to a large mixing bowl.

Place the butter in a large saucepan and cook over low heat until it melts. Gradually add the flour, salt, and white pepper, stirring all the time. As soon as it thickens, gradually add the milk, whisking constantly until it has the consistency of heavy cream, 3 to 4 minutes. Gradually add the cheeses, stirring all the time. Add the cheese mixture to the pasta, stir to combine, and set aside 20 minutes.

Meanwhile, preheat the oven to 350 degrees F. Stir the pasta again and transfer to a 9 x 13-inch baking dish.

*To make the topping:* Place the Parmesan, cheddar, bread crumbs, and butter in a small bowl and mix well. Then sprinkle evenly over the pasta. (You can cover and refrigerate up to 2 days or freeze up to 3 months.)

Transfer to the oven and bake until golden brown, 35 to 40 minutes.

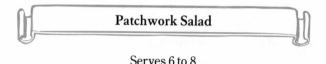

## Patchwork Salad

Serves 6 to 8

¼ cup plain yogurt

¼ cup mayonnaise

¼ cup Dijon mustard

½ teaspoon kosher salt

¼ teaspoon black pepper

2 small zucchini, cut in large dice

4 carrots, cut in large dice

8 small red radishes, halved and sliced

1 pint cherry tomatoes, halved

¼ cup chopped fresh Italian flat-leaf parsley

1 avocado, diced

Place the yogurt, mayonnaise, mustard, salt, and pepper in a large bowl and mix well. Add the zucchini, carrots, radishes, tomatoes, and parsley and mix well. Add the avocado, gently mix, and serve immediately.

## Chocolate Zucchini Bread

Yield: 8 to 10 slices

1 cup light brown sugar, loosely packed

2 large eggs, at room temperature

½ cup (1 stick) unsalted butter, melted, or ½ cup canola oil

1½ cups grated zucchini

1 teaspoon vanilla extract

1¼ cups all-purpose flour

½ cup unsweetened cocoa powder

1½ teaspoons baking soda

½ teaspoon kosher salt

Preheat the oven to 350 degrees F. Lightly grease a 9 x 5 x 5-inch loaf pan.

Place the sugar, eggs, and butter in the bowl of a mixer fitted with a paddle and beat until thickened, 2 to 3 minutes. Add the zucchini and vanilla and beat until well incorporated. Combine the dry ingredients and add to the batter, about ½ cup at a time, mixing to combine. (If you don't do this gradually, the cocoa powder will be everywhere.)

Pour into the prepared pan, transfer to the oven, and bake until deep brown and firm, 50 minutes to 1 hour.

## Quilt Block Cookies
### (Sugar Cookie with Sugar Icing Decoration)

Yield: 3 to 4 dozen cookies

For the cookies:

1 cup (2 sticks) unsalted butter,
   at room temperature
¾ cup sugar
1 large egg, at room temperature
1 teaspoon vanilla extract
2¼ cups all-purpose flour
½ teaspoon baking powder
¼ teaspoon kosher salt

For the icing:

2 cups confectioners' sugar
¼ cup very hot tap water
½ teaspoon corn syrup
¼ teaspoon vanilla extract
   or lemon extract

Assortment of colored sugars, for decoration

*To make the cookies:* Place the butter and sugar in a mixer fitted with a paddle and process until creamy. Add the egg and vanilla and mix until the egg is incorporated. Add the flour, baking powder, and salt and mix until the mixture comes together. Remove from the bowl and form into a log, cover with parchment or wax paper, and refrigerate 1 hour.

Remove the log from the refrigerator and form into a 1½ x 1½-inch squared column. Return to the refrigerator and chill at least 2 hours and up to 1 week.

When you are ready to bake the cookies, preheat the oven to 350 degrees F.

Cut slices ¼ inch thick and place on a baking sheet lined with parchment paper.

Bake for 10 to 12 minutes. Remove from the pan and cool before decorating.

*To make the icing:* Place all the ingredients in a small bowl and whisk until smooth. Using a small pastry brush, paint the cooled cookies with icing, then sprinkle each quadrant with a different colored sugar.

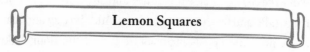

## Lemon Squares

Yield: 16 squares

For the crust:

1 cup all-purpose flour

⅓ cup sugar

¼ teaspoon kosher salt

½ cup (1 stick) unsalted butter, chilled and chopped

For the filling:

1 cup sugar

½ cup heavy cream

2 large eggs, at room temperature

1 tablespoon cornstarch

½ teaspoon vanilla extract

¼ teaspoon kosher salt

Zest and juice of 2 lemons

Preheat the oven to 350 degrees F. Lightly butter or line with parchment paper an 8 x 8-inch pan.

*To make the crust:* Place the flour, sugar, and salt in the bowl of a food processor fitted with a steel blade and process until well combined. While the machine is running, drop pieces of butter into the flour and combine until the mixture resembles cornmeal. Press into the prepared pan, transfer to the oven, and bake until golden, about 22 minutes. Set aside to cool.

*To make the filling:* Place all the ingredients in a bowl and whisk until well combined. Pour into the cooled crust, transfer to the oven, and bake until golden, still at 350 degrees, about 25 minutes. Cool to room temperature, cover, and refrigerate at least 2 hours and up to overnight. Cut into 16 squares.

## Pineapple Upside-Down Cake

Serves 8 to 10

6 tablespoons plus ½ cup (1 stick)
    unsalted butter
One 20-ounce can pineapple rings, drained
¾ cup light brown sugar, loosely packed
1½ cups all-purpose flour
1 teaspoon baking powder
½ teaspoon kosher salt
1 cup sugar
2 large eggs

1 teaspoon vanilla extract

½ cup whole milk

Preheat the oven to 350 degrees F. Grease a 9-inch round cake pan.

Place the 6 tablespoons butter in a small saucepan and cook over medium heat until melted. Add the brown sugar and stir until the mixture is smooth. Pour into the pan. Arrange 7 pineapple rings in the bottom of the prepared pan. Cut the 3 remaining pineapple rings in half and press the half rings evenly spaced along the side of the pan, cut side facing up.

Combine the flour, baking powder, and salt in a medium bowl.

Place the remaining 8 tablespoons butter and sugar in the bowl of a stand mixer fitted with a paddle and mix on medium-high speed until light and fluffy, 2 to 3 minutes. Add the eggs, one at a time, and mix until combined. Add half the dry ingredients and mix until just combined. Add the vanilla extract and milk and mix until combined. Add the remaining dry ingredients and mix until smooth and fluffy. Pour the batter over the pineapple and spread in an even layer. Transfer to the oven and bake until a toothpick inserted in the center of the cake comes out with a few moist crumbs, 40 to 45 minutes.

Let the cake cool in the pan for 5 minutes, then run a knife around the perimeter and turn it out onto a cake plate. Cool completely before serving.

### Bee Tea

Serves 8

2 tablespoons loose black tea
2 tablespoons loose green tea
1 tablespoon loose chamomile tea
2 tablespoons honey
Lemon quarters or whole milk

Place the teas in a teapot and cover with about 8 cups boiling water. Let steep 4 minutes and then remove the tea. Add honey and stir well. Serve immediately with lemon quarters or milk (but not both).

# CHAPTER THREE

# National Quilting Day

 "As much as I'd appreciate our friends' help today," said Sylvia, rising stiffly and brushing off the seat of her trousers, "this is not the time to have a quilting bee, or cleaning-up-the-kitchen bee, or any other sort of bee for that matter."

"Why not?" asked Anna.

Sylvia took a glass from a cupboard, filled it at the sink, and took a sip of water. "Because as you said, we couldn't have a bee without refreshments, and not even a chef as skilled as you could feed a crowd from a kitchen in such disarray."

"You'd be surprised." Anna thanked Sylvia as she filled a second glass and passed it across the counter to her. Anna hadn't really exerted herself enough to work up a thirst, but she appreciated the gesture. "The kitchen in my apartment is only a fraction of the size of yours, and I've turned out some rather impressive meals there, if I do say so myself. Ask Jeremy. He's been my taste-tester ever since he moved in across the hall."

Sylvia finished her water and placed her glass in the sink. "You don't need to bring in witnesses, dear. I have absolute faith in your ability to create a gourmet meal using nothing more than a saucepan and a hot plate."

If Sylvia only knew that Anna's home kitchen boasted little more than that. Her kitchen—or kitchenette, as it said on her lease—was wholly inappropriate for a chef: It was no bigger than a walk-in closet, with a small refrigerator, a single sink, a two-burner electric stovetop, and an oven too small to accommodate her jelly-roll pan. But at least both burners gave consistent heat, which was more than could be said for Sylvia's stove. Anna couldn't wait for the eight-burner gas stove to be installed. She would be in heaven, absolute heaven.

"What can you whip up in this?" Sylvia asked, gesturing to the small microwave that bore an uncanny resemblance to the Easy-Bake Oven Anna had received for Christmas as a child. She wondered if it, too, cooked with a lightbulb.

Anna checked the wattage, opened the door, closed it, and shook her head. "I don't know. I really don't think it's good for much more than heating up cups of coffee and melting butter."

"It's all we're going to have for quite a while," Sylvia

warned. "Until our new appliances and countertops arrive, we're going to have to learn to cook with this, or get by on cold cereal, sandwiches, and takeout."

"Not at all," said Anna, surprised. "We'll ask the contractors to plug in the fridge in the dining room for our perishables, I'll use the old kitchen table for prep work, and I'll fix our meals in your slow cooker."

Sylvia nodded, thoughtful. "I hadn't considered that, but I'm certainly glad you did. I wasn't looking forward to a month of cornflakes, pizza, and kung pao."

A month? Anna hoped Sylvia had added two weeks to the estimate either in error or to be conservative, and not because the contractor had already begun warning of delays. "If we stay on schedule, we should be cooking in here in two weeks," she said, relieved when Sylvia didn't contradict her. "I have enough slow-cooker recipes to last us that long. We'll have so much variety that you'll forget we have no oven."

"If we explain our situation to the other Elm Creek Quilters, I'm sure they'll share their recipes," Sylvia said. "I've sampled several of their meals on past National Quilting Days—Summer's vegetarian chili, Bonnie's chicken and dumplings. Delicious."

"National Quilting Day?" echoed Anna. "Is that an Elm Creek Quilts invention? I thought it was always National Quilting Day around here."

"Oh, we can't take credit for it. The National Quilting Association started it in 1991."

Anna couldn't believe it. "You're kidding. There really is such a holiday?"

"Of course," said Sylvia, pretending to be astounded that Anna hadn't known. "Why not? What better way to spend the third Saturday in March every year but in celebration of the art and history of quilting?"

"I can't think of anything," said Anna, laughing and holding up her hands in defense. "The only real question is why National Quilting Day wasn't established centuries ago. It should be right up there with Thanksgiving and . . . Arbor Day."

"Arbor Day?" Sylvia laughed and shook her head. "We'll let our caretaker organize that celebration. As for the Elm Creek Quilters, we've created our own traditions. National Quilting Day happens to fall right before quilt camp begins its new season. As you can imagine, that's a very busy time of year for our staff. A few years ago, we decided to make National Quilting Day a collaborative workday here at the manor. On that Saturday, the Elm Creek Quilters gather to consult with one another about lesson plans and schedules, to plan for the months ahead, and to finish up class sample projects. But of course no one can spare time to fix supper, so in the morning before the others arrive, Sarah and I put together a tasty dish in the slow cooker, or one of our friends brings her slow cooker filled and ready to plug in. Others bring beverages, munchies, or desserts. We work hard all day, enjoying our camaraderie and the anticipation of the new camp season, and we never fail to accomplish a great deal of work. And then, at the end of the day, we share a delicious meal that has been cooking all day, filling the kitchen with delightful aromas."

Anna thought the tradition sounded like a wonderful way to begin a new year of quilt camp. She imagined the Elm Creek Quilters sitting around the old wooden table that had once taken up half Sylvia's kitchen—seated side by side on the wooden benches, passing dishes around, complimenting the cooks, teasing, joking, worrying, reassuring, solving problems, and making plans. But she did not see herself among those gathered at the table.

The founding members of the circle of quilters had known one another so well for so long. Together they had struggled through tough times and had celebrated wonderful achievements. Was there room at their table for a newcomer?

She would find a way in, Anna told herself. Even if the benches were filled, she could always pull up a chair at one end of the table or the other.

"This National Quilting Day, you and Sarah should focus on quilting, which I know you enjoy more than cooking," said

Anna. "I'll take care of supper and snacks, and I'll use the slow cooker even after our kitchen is in working order, in honor of your tradition."

"An excellent plan," said Sylvia. "That way you don't have to spend your day in the kitchen, either, but can keep the rest of us company, and perhaps even whip up a quilt or two."

"However I can help out," said Anna. She'd make supper, class samples, photocopies—anything that was needed. Whatever it took to earn her place among the Elm Creek Quilters, she would do.

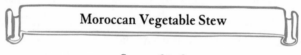

**Moroccan Vegetable Stew**

Serves 6 to 8

For the stew:

1 tablespoon olive oil

2 large leeks, washed well and chopped

1 tablespoon chopped fresh gingerroot

3 garlic cloves, thinly sliced

½ teaspoon ground cinnamon

¼ teaspoon cayenne pepper

1 teaspoon curry powder

2 parsnips, diced

4 carrots, diced

1 butternut squash, diced (5 to 6 cups)

3 zucchini, diced

One 14.5-ounce can diced tomatoes, drained

5 to 6 cups vegetable broth

¼ cup chopped fresh Italian flat-leaf parsley or basil leaves,
    for garnish

Grated zest of 1 lemon, for garnish

Place a large stockpot over medium heat and when it is hot, add the oil. Add the leeks, ginger, garlic, cinnamon, cayenne, and curry powder and cook until tender, 10 to 15 minutes. Add the parsnips, carrots, and squash and cook, stirring occasionally, for 10 minutes. Keep at medium heat and add the zucchini, tomatoes, and vegetable broth and bring just to a boil. Reduce the heat to low and cook, partially covered, until the vegetables are tender but do not fall apart, about 45 minutes to 1 hour.

Serve immediately with steamed basmati rice or transfer to a container, cover, and refrigerate up to 2 days. Garnish with parsley and lemon zest.

## Pot Roast and Potatoes

Serves 6 to 8

5½- to 6-pound piece of brisket

2 tablespoons kosher salt

1 tablespoon black pepper

1 tablespoon olive or vegetable oil

6 garlic cloves, chopped

3 large Spanish onions, halved and chopped

2 cups dry red wine

One 6-ounce can tomato paste

3 to 4 cups water, as needed

2 tablespoons light brown sugar

1½ pounds carrots, peeled and cut in large chunks

3 medium russet potatoes, peeled and cut in large chunks

2 tablespoons fresh lemon juice

Chopped fresh Italian flat-leaf parsley, for garnish

Pat the brisket dry with paper towels and season with salt and pepper.

Place a Dutch oven over high heat and when it is hot, add the oil. Add the brisket and cook until seared on all sides, about 10 minutes in all. Set the brisket aside.

Reheat on medium high, add the garlic and onions, and cook until soft and slightly golden, 10 to 15 minutes, stirring often. Add the red wine and cook 2 minutes. Stir in the tomato paste.

Preheat the oven to 325 degrees F.

Return the brisket to the Dutch oven, fat side up. Add the water and brown sugar at the edge of the pan. Bring the mixture to a light boil, cover, transfer to the oven, and cook 1½ hours.

Add the carrots and potatoes. The vegetables should be submerged in water; add more water, if necessary. Cover the Dutch oven and continue cooking until the meat and vegetables are very tender, about 1 hour.

Remove the brisket from the Dutch oven and defat the liquid. Meanwhile, cut the brisket across the grain into thin slices (about ⅛ inch thick). Return the brisket to the Dutch oven. Combine with the lemon juice and serve immediately, garnished with parsley.

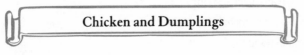

## Chicken and Dumplings

Serves 6 to 8

For the stew:

4 to 5 pounds bone-in skin-on chicken thighs or breasts or a combination, dried with a paper towel

1½ teaspoons kosher salt

½ teaspoon black pepper

4 carrots, chopped

2 celery stalks, chopped

1 large Spanish onion, chopped

¼ cup all-purpose flour

2 teaspoons dried thyme

2 bay leaves

8 cups chicken broth

¼ cup dry sherry

1 cup frozen peas

¼ cup light or heavy cream

¼ cup chopped fresh Italian flat-leaf parsley, for garnish

### For the dumplings:

½ cup whole milk

1 tablespoon unsalted butter, melted

1 cup all-purpose flour

1½ teaspoons baking powder

½ teaspoon kosher salt

*To make the stew*: Sprinkle the chicken with the salt and pepper. Place a Dutch oven over medium-high heat and when it is hot, add the chicken, skin side down, and sear until well browned, about 4 minutes per side. Using tongs, remove the chicken and set aside on a plate. When cool enough to handle, remove and discard the skin.

Pour off all but 2 tablespoons fat. Reduce the heat to low, add the carrots, celery, and onion and cook until the vegetables are soft and golden, 10 to 15 minutes. Add the flour, thyme, and bay leaves and stir constantly for 2 minutes. Very gradually, add the chicken broth and sherry, and bring to a low boil. Return the chicken to the Dutch oven and cook, turning the chicken halfway, until the meat falls away from the bones, about 45 minutes. Remove the chicken and set aside until it is cool enough to handle. Remove the bay leaves. Take the meat off the bones and return the meat to the Dutch oven. Cool, then skim off and discard the fat. Cover and refrigerate overnight.

*To make the dumplings:* Place the milk and butter in a medium-size bowl and stir well. Add the remaining ingredients and mix to combine. Divide into 16 balls of equal size and flatten slightly.

Reheat the stew over medium heat until warmed throughout, about 10 minutes. Gently add the dumplings to the simmering stew and cook until they have increased in size, about 15 minutes. Add the peas and cream and cook until heated through, about 3 minutes. Serve, garnished with the parsley.

## BBQ Pork Sandwiches (Slow Cooker)

Serves 8 to 10

For the rub:

1 tablespoon kosher salt

1 tablespoon sugar

1 tablespoon light brown sugar

1 tablespoon ground cumin

1 tablespoon chili powder

1 tablespoon Hungarian paprika

2 teaspoons black pepper

½ teaspoon cayenne pepper

For the pork:

4 pounds pork butt, cut into 4 chunks

2 tablespoons canola oil

For the sauce:

One 28-ounce can diced tomatoes, with liquid

2½ cups water

¾ cup cider vinegar

½ cup light brown sugar, loosely packed

2 tablespoons tomato paste

3 garlic cloves, minced

1 bay leaf

2 teaspoons ground cumin

1 teaspoon kosher salt

½ teaspoon black pepper

½ teaspoon crushed red pepper flakes

8 hamburger or other soft rolls

Barbecue sauce (optional)

*To make the rub:* Place the salt, sugars, cumin, chili powder, paprika, black pepper, and cayenne in a bowl and mix well. Dredge the pork butt in the rub and massage into the meat. Cover tightly with plastic wrap and refrigerate at least 4 hours or up to 2 days. Let the meat come to room temperature before cooking, about 1 hour.

*To make the sauce:* Place the tomatoes, water, cider vinegar, brown sugar, tomato paste, garlic, bay leaf, cumin, salt, pepper and red pepper flakes in a slow cooker and cook according to the manufacturer's instructions (or in a medium-size saucepan over medium-low heat) for 1½ hours. This can be made up to 2 days ahead of time.

*To cook the pork:* Place a large skillet over medium-high heat and when it is hot, add the oil. Add the pork, one piece at a time, allowing the pan to reheat between additions, and brown on all sides. Transfer to a plate.

Combine the sauce and pork in a slow cooker and cook according to the manufacturer's instructions (or in a medium-size saucepan over medium-low heat) until the meat is fork tender, about 4 hours. Remove the meat from the pan and degrease the sauce. When the meat has cooled somewhat, shred it with your hands and return to the degreased liquid. Reheat over low heat. Place big scoops on the buns and serve immediately, with extra barbecue sauce, if desired.

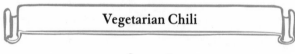

## Vegetarian Chili

### Serves 8

2 tablespoons olive or canola oil

2 Spanish onions, coarsely chopped

4 garlic cloves, finely chopped

2 red bell peppers, coarsely chopped

1 small eggplant, peeled (if desired), and cubed

2 small zucchini, cubed

1 tablespoon dried Greek oregano

1 to 2 tablespoons red pepper powder

2 teaspoons crushed red pepper flakes

2 teaspoons ground cumin, or more to taste

1 teaspoon cayenne pepper (optional)

One 15–15.5-ounce can or 2 cups cooked white beans,
    drained and rinsed

One 15–15.5-ounce can or 2 cups cooked black beans,
    drained and rinsed

Four (15–15.5-ounce) cans dark red kidney beans,
    drained and rinsed

One 15–15.5-ounce can garbanzo beans, drained and rinsed

1 cup dried brown lentils, picked over and rinsed

Two 28-ounce cans diced or whole tomatoes, coarsely
    chopped, including juice

Freshly chopped cilantro or basil leaves, for garnish

Lime quarters, for garnish

Place a large stockpot over medium-low heat and when it is hot, add the oil. Add the onions, garlic, peppers, eggplant, zucchini, and spices and cook until the vegetables have softened, about 10 minutes.

Add the beans, lentils, and tomatoes and cook, covered, for 1 to 2 hours, stirring occasionally. If the chili begins to boil, lower the heat. Cover and refrigerate in a storage container overnight.

Reheat and garnish with the basil or cilantro and serve with lime quarters.

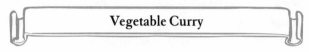

## Vegetable Curry

### Serves 4 to 6

2 tablespoons olive oil

1 Spanish or red onion, chopped

4 garlic cloves, minced

¼ cup curry powder

2 large zucchini, diced

1 yellow squash, diced

1 red bell pepper, diced

2 Granny Smith apples, cored, peeled, and diced

2 cups diced tomatoes, canned or fresh

½ cup mango chutney

Fresh cilantro leaves, for garnish

Yogurt, for garnish

Place a medium-size stockpot over medium-low heat and when it is hot, add the oil. Add the onion and garlic and cook 10 minutes. Add the curry powder, zucchini, and squash, cover, and cook 10 minutes. Add the red pepper and apples and cook, covered, for 10 minutes. Add the tomatoes and chutney and cook, uncovered, for 10 minutes, if the tomatoes are canned, and 20 minutes, if fresh.

Cover and refrigerate overnight or serve immediately, garnished with cilantro leaves and yogurt.

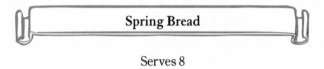

## Spring Bread

Serves 8

This recipe is from Jennifer's husband's grandmother, Giuditta Chiaverini, and has been a family favorite for many years.

    1 large cake yeast, broken up, or 1 package active dry yeast
        (0.25 ounces = 2¼ teaspoons)
    2 cups warm water
    1½ cups sugar
    6 large eggs or 12 egg whites (for low-cholesterol diets)
    1 cup canola or olive oil
    2 tablespoons (1 ounce) anise extract
    7 to 7 ½ cups unbleached flour
    Butter or olive oil for rubbing on finished loaves

Place the yeast and water in a large bowl and mix well. Add the sugar and stir well. Combine the eggs, oil, and anise extract and stir again. Add the flour, gradually, and stir until it is no longer sticky and can be handled easily.

Place the dough on a floured surface and knead until smooth and elastic, 15 to 20 minutes.

Spray a large bowl with nonstick cooking spray. Place the dough in the bowl and cover with kitchen towels. Let rise in a warm place until doubled in size, about 1½ hours. Knead again for a few minutes and then divide the dough into softball-size shapes.

At this point, you can use your imagination. You can place in free-form shapes on a baking sheet sprayed with nonstick cooking spray, in loaf pans, or five balls in a tube pan nestled close together (my favorite way to bake this bread). If you use the tube pan, the balls should be smaller than a softball (just big enough to nestle together without crowding). You will have dough left over, which can be shaped as you wish. After placing the dough on a baking sheet, cover, and set aside to rise until doubled in size, about 1 to 1½ hours.

Preheat the oven to 350 degrees F.

Transfer the dough to the oven and bake until golden brown, about 35 minutes, depending upon the size of the loaf. You can use the "thump" method to test doneness. When the bread looks golden brown, "thump" it with your knuckle, and if it sounds hollow, it is ready to be removed from the oven. Cool the bread enough to remove from the pan. While still warm, to make the crust shiny, rub lightly with butter or olive oil.

## Sweet and Spicy Nuts

Yield: 4 cups

1 large egg white, lightly beaten
2 tablespoons cold water
½ cup sugar
½ teaspoon kosher salt
½ teaspoon ground cinnamon
¼ teaspoon ground ginger
¼ to ½ teaspoon chili powder
4 cups raw pecans or walnuts

Preheat the oven to 250 degrees F. Line a baking sheet with parchment paper.

Place the egg white, water, sugar, salt, and spices in a large bowl and mix well. Add the nuts to the mixture and toss until well coated. Pour onto the prepared sheet and arrange in a single layer.

Transfer to the oven and bake, stirring every 15 minutes, until the pecans appear dry, about 1 hour and 15 minutes. Immediately loosen the nuts with a spatula and set aside to cool.

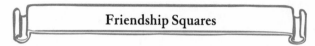

## Friendship Squares

Yield: 24 squares

1 cup (2 sticks) unsalted butter

5 ounces unsweetened chocolate, coarsely chopped

2 cups sugar

4 large eggs, at room temperature

2 teaspoons vanilla extract

¾ cup all-purpose flour

½ teaspoon kosher salt

½ cup chopped walnuts

1 cup chocolate chips

½ cup shredded coconut

Preheat the oven to 325 degrees F. Lightly grease and flour a 9 x 13-inch pan.

Place the butter and chocolate in a small metal bowl set over a pot of gently simmering water. Stir occasionally until the chocolate is melted and the mixture is smooth. Set aside until slightly thickened and cool to the touch, 20 to 30 minutes.

Place the sugar and eggs in the bowl of a stand mixer fitted with a paddle and mix until thick and creamy. Add the vanilla and mix well. Scrape down the sides of the bowl, add the flour, melted chocolate, and salt and mix until just combined. Pour the mixture into the prepared pan.

Sprinkle the top with the walnuts, chocolate chips, and coconut. Transfer to the oven and bake until a tester comes out clean, 25 to 30 minutes. Set aside to cool on a wire rack.

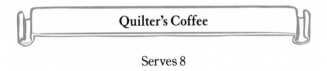

### Quilter's Coffee

Serves 8

4 cups freshly brewed coffee
3 cups warm milk
1 teaspoon ground cinnamon
½ teaspoon ground ginger

Place all the ingredients in a medium-size pot, whisking all the while, and heat until hot. Serve immediately.

# CHAPTER FOUR

# Picnic on the Veranda

 "National Quilting Day always feels like the first day of spring to me," Sylvia remarked. "Even if a crust of snow still lingers on the ground, on the third Saturday of March I always feel as if spring is dawning and summer is just around the corner."

Anna was about to reply when, upon opening a low cupboard near the side window, she caught the unmistakable whiff of mildew. "Sylvia, you might have some water damage here." She pulled on a pair of rubber gloves before reaching deeper into the cupboard. "I think the window seal leaked."

"It's little wonder, considering that the windows haven't been updated since the Roaring Twenties." Sylvia set a cookie sheet aside with a clatter and came over to inspect the damage for herself. "Perhaps we should have the contractor add replacement windows to the project. Summer has been after me for years to make the manor more energy efficient."

"We might as well do it all at once," Anna agreed, ruefully adding another few days to her mental calendar. If mold or mildew had settled in the walls—

When her gloved hand touched folded cloth, she grasped hold and pulled a bundle of faded, red-and-white gingham fabric into the open. Anna wrinkled her nose and turned her head away as the unpleasant odor intensified. "I think I found our mildew problem."

"Oh, my goodness." Sylvia rested her hand upon the counter and wisely came no closer. "How many times did I tell my sister never to put that tablecloth away wet? She never would take my advice."

"This was a tablecloth?" Anna gingerly unfolded one blackened, deteriorating edge, trying to imagine that it had once been suitable to serve food upon. To her surprise she found that the center of the tablecloth had been spared from the mildew, and the cheerful red-and-white checks were not as faded.

"I haven't seen that old tablecloth in more than fifty years," said Sylvia. "It's remarkable that even a thread of it is left. It saw hard use through the years, ever since my grandmother Elizabeth brought it home from the old dry goods store on Church Street in Waterford. It served as our tablecloth when we ate supper out on the veranda on sunny summer days and as our picnic blanket when we ate lunch beneath the elms on the banks of Elm Creek. When my younger brother was just a baby, my mother used to take us out nearly every day in fair weather. He would play on this tablecloth with my mother while my sister and I ran and picked flowers and threw pebbles into the creek." Sylvia shook her head in wonder, gazing at the worn red-and-white gingham fondly. "Such memories I have of meals shared over this tablecloth—and stories, too. Old stories about the manor, of course, the tales about the first Bergstroms to come to America that my siblings and I knew well and loved—but mostly stories about my parents' and grandparents' childhoods. There's something about a picnic that brings out lighthearted tales, don't you agree?"

Anna hesitated, not wishing to disagree with Sylvia and spoil her fond reminiscence. For Anna, nothing about family meals, picnics or otherwise, evoked thoughts of lighthearted stories and little girls picking flowers. Meals with the Del Maso family involved lots of food and wine, boisterous laughter, and intense conversations that often flared into heated arguments, which turned into rounds of teasing when the anger was spent. Extra places were always set in anticipation of the neighbors, friends, and extended family who might show up unexpectedly to debate politics with her father or gossip about absent acquaintances with her mother. And Anna had loved it, even when she had to shout to make her opinions heard over her brothers' deeper voices, even when the people she loved best in the world drove her crazy. Those happy hours spent around her family's kitchen table were surely what had inspired her to become a chef. She only wished she could reproduce the spirit of those occasions as deftly as she had captured the flavors of her mother's and grandmothers' traditional recipes. From the look in Sylvia's eyes, she knew Sylvia felt the same way about her own family's traditions, even though the spirit of those two very different families were surely equally different.

"Lighthearted doesn't describe my family or their stories very well," Anna said. "Intense, yes. Passionate, definitely. Happy, of course. But there was never anything easygoing and relaxed about us, and I think we liked it that way."

Anna imagined her parents and siblings and cousins and aunts and uncles gathered for a picnic on the veranda, just as the quilt campers had done throughout the last weeks of summer, Anna's first as Elm Creek Manor's chef. The campers had enjoyed fried chicken and sandwich wraps, tasty salads, fruit, and cupcakes for dessert. They had chatted pleasantly, laughed, and teased one another. As for the Del Maso family, no meal was complete without a huge bowl of pasta in the center of the table, and the decibel level would have soared high above whatever the quilters could have produced.

But she smiled, imagining both groups of picnickers meeting on the veranda. The quilters would surely wonder why the

Del Masos were shouting and gesturing, giving every appearance of discord. Unless the quilters came from large Italian families themselves, they would probably be completely unaware that the Del Masos were thoroughly enjoying themselves, that every teasing retort was an expression of love.

"I don't suppose any amount of bleach and hot water will make this tablecloth usable again," Sylvia said with a small, regretful sigh. "Such a pity. Our campers love picnics on the veranda, and this tablecloth would have added such a lovely note of nostalgia. It would have made those occasions even more special for me."

Anna knew exactly what she meant. A table adorned with familiar linens and china evoked family traditions just as familiar flavors did. If the gingham tablecloth could somehow be restored . . . "The fabric in the center looks salvageable," she said, indicating a section free of water stains and mildew, where the red-and-white checks remained cheerful and bright. "If we washed it well, trimmed away the ruined parts, and hemmed the edges, it could work."

"Perhaps as a table runner, but not as a tablecloth." Sylvia shook her head, but then she paused, thoughtful. "Perhaps a table runner would suffice. Let's not discard it yet. Set it aside, and when we've finished our remodeling and we're ready for another project, we'll see what we can do with it. I can't bear to throw it out, not if we can preserve at least some portion of it."

Anna nodded, picked up the tablecloth gingerly, and placed it in the hallway to air out where the odor of mildew wouldn't bother them. She knew Sylvia cared more about preserving the memories of summer picnics than saving the fabric itself, but the red-and-white gingham evoked those memories the way nothing else could.

Even if only a table runner remained, something of that tablecloth had to be preserved. Anna didn't know how, but she knew that when she told the other Elm Creek Quilters how much it mattered to Sylvia, they would come up with a solution. The circle of quilters would not fail their friend.

## Fried Chicken

### Serves 6 to 8

8 skinless, boneless chicken thighs, trimmed of fat

2 cups buttermilk

1 teaspoon Tabasco (optional)

For the coating:

1 cup all-purpose flour

2 teaspoons kosher salt

1 teaspoon black pepper

½ teaspoon cayenne pepper

½ teaspoon dried thyme

2 large eggs

¼ cup water

Canola oil

Lemon wedges, for garnish

Place the chicken, buttermilk, and if desired, the Tabasco in a bowl, mix well, cover, and refrigerate overnight.

Drain the chicken and dry it as well as possible.

Place the flour, salt, pepper, cayenne, and thyme on a plate and mix well. Place the eggs and water on a plate and mix well.

Dredge the chicken in the flour mixture, being sure to coat the chicken completely and shaking off any excess. Dip the chicken in the eggs and then again in the flour mixture. Shake off any excess, cover, and refrigerate 1 to 2 hours.

Place enough oil in a large deep skillet so that it reaches about ½ inch high. Heat the oil to 350 to 375 degrees F over medium-high heat. This will take about 7 minutes but you must use a thermometer. When the oil is hot, add the chicken pieces one at a time, making sure the oil reheats before adding each piece. Cook each piece until deep golden brown, 5 to 8 minutes.

Using tongs, remove the chicken to a paper towel. Serve immediately with lemon wedges.

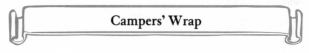

**Campers' Wrap**

Serves 8

8 white or whole-wheat wraps, pitas, or soft-flour tortillas
¾ pound Virginia baked ham, thinly sliced
½ pound Brie cheese, sliced
½ cup honey mustard
2 firm pears, cored and thinly sliced
8 romaine leaves
1 teaspoon kosher salt
½ teaspoon black pepper

Divide and layer the ingredients evenly among the 8 wraps and tightly roll. Serve immediately or cover and refrigerate up to 4 hours.

## Three-Bean Salad

Serves 4

For the salad:

1 cup cooked or canned dark red kidney beans,
    drained and rinsed
1 cup cooked or canned black turtle beans,
    drained and rinsed
1 cup cooked or canned white or garbanzo beans,
    drained and rinsed
2 cups green beans, trimmed and snapped in half
½ bunch scallions, root end and 1-inch green part
    trimmed and discarded, remainder chopped
¼ cup fresh Italian flat-leaf parsley,
    coarsely chopped

For the dressing:

2 garlic cloves
2 tablespoons red wine vinegar
1 tablespoon Dijon mustard
¼ cup olive oil

½ cup fesh basil

Kosher salt and black pepper

*To make the salad:* Place the beans, scallions, and parsley in a medium-size mixing bowl and toss to combine. Set aside.

*To make the dressing:* Place the garlic in a food processor or blender and pulse until the garlic is chopped. Add the vinegar, mustard, olive oil, and basil and mix until well combined. Add to the bowl of beans, toss well, adding salt and pepper to taste. Cover and refrigerate at least 2 hours and up to overnight before serving.

## Vermicelli Salad

Serves 4 to 6

3 garlic cloves

1 cup fresh basil leaves

2 tablespoons fresh lemon juice

2 tablespoons warm water

3 tablespoons olive oil

1 pound vermicelli, cooked according to package directions, drained, and slightly cooled

¼ cup lightly toasted pine nuts or chopped walnuts

2 tomatoes, diced

¼ cup chopped black kalamata olives

½ to ¾ cup grated Parmesan cheese

Place the garlic in the bowl of a food processor fitted with a steel blade and pulse to chop. Add ½ cup of the basil leaves and process until chopped. While the machine is running, add the lemon juice and water and process. Add the olive oil and process until very smooth. Pour over the vermicelli and toss well. Add the remaining ingredients. Serve immediately or cover and refrigerate up to 4 hours. Garnish with the remaining ½ cup basil.

**Southwestern Couscous, Corn, and Black Bean Salad**

Yield: 5 to 6 cups

For the salad:

½ cup boiling water

¾ cup couscous

2 cups raw corn kernels

One 15–15.5-ounce can black turtle beans,
    drained and rinsed
1 cup chopped seeded plum tomatoes
¼ cup chopped red onion
1 teaspoon kosher salt, or more, to taste

For the dressing:

¼ cup olive oil
2 tablespoons fresh lemon or lime juice
¼ cup chopped fresh cilantro leaves
2 large garlic cloves, crushed or minced
¼ teaspoon crushed red pepper flakes (optional)
½ to 1 teaspoon kosher salt

*To make the salad:* Place the water and couscous in a small bowl and cover. Let sit 5 minutes.

Place the remaining ingredients in a large mixing bowl, add the couscous, and mix to combine.

*To make the dressing:* Put all the ingredients in a small bowl and whisk well. Add the dressing to the couscous-corn mixture, cover, and refrigerate at least 2 hours and up to overnight. Serve chilled or at room temperature.

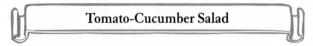

## Tomato-Cucumber Salad

Yield: about 7 cups

4 cups chopped tomatoes
1 English cucumber, cut in large dice
2 tablespoons chopped fresh basil leaves
¼ cup olive oil
2 tablespoons balsamic vinegar
1 teaspoon kosher salt
¼ teaspoon black pepper

Place all the ingredients in a large serving bowl, gently toss, and serve immediately.

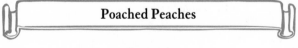

## Poached Peaches

Serves 4

1 cup dry white wine
½ cup water
⅓ cup sugar

1 vanilla bean, split lengthwise

4 firm but ripe peaches, halved or cut into thick slices

Place the wine, water, sugar, and vanilla bean in a medium-size saucepan and bring to a boil over high heat. Lower the heat and simmer, stirring occasionally, until the sugar has dissolved. Off the heat, remove the vanilla bean and scrape the seed back into the syrup. Return to medium heat, add the peaches, and simmer until the peaches are just tender, 10 to 12 minutes.

Transfer to a bowl and refrigerate until cold, at least 3 hours.

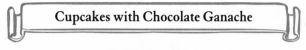

## Cupcakes with Chocolate Ganache

Yield: 12 cupcakes

For the ganache:

1 cup heavy cream

8 ounces semisweet chocolate, chopped

For the cupcakes:

1½ cups all-purpose flour

1½ teaspoons baking powder

½ teaspoon kosher salt

½ cup (1 stick) unsalted butter, at room temperature

1 cup sugar

1 large egg, at room temperature

2 large egg yolks, at room temperature

1½ teaspoons vanilla extract

½ cup sour cream

Preheat the oven to 350 degrees. Line 12-cup muffin pan with paper or foil liners.

*To make the ganache:* Place the heavy cream in a small saucepan over medium-high heat and cook until it just comes to a boil, 3 to 4 minutes. Place the chocolate in a medium-size bowl and add the cream. Cover the bowl with aluminum foil or a plate and set aside for 5 minutes. Stir until smooth. Cover and refrigerate until it has cooled completely, 45 minutes to 1 hour.

*To prepare the cupcakes:* Place the ingredients in a bowl and mix, by hand or with a mixer fitted with a paddle, until smooth and satiny (about 30 seconds with the mixer). Scrape down the sides of the bowl and mix again until smooth.

Divide the batter evenly among the 12 cups. Transfer the muffin pan to the oven and bake until the tops are just beginning to color but not brown, 20 to 24 minutes.

Transfer the cupcakes to a wire rack and set aside to cool. When the cupcakes and the ganache have fully cooled, *finish the ganache:* Using a hand-held mixer or a stand mixer fitted with a whisk attachment, whip the chocolate until it is light brown and fluffy and forms medium-stiff peaks, about 2 minutes.

Place 2 to 3 generous tablespoons on each cupcake and spread until smooth.

## Dutch Apple Pie

Serves 8

For the crust:

3 cups all-purpose flour
1 teaspoon sugar
¾ teaspoon kosher salt
¾ cup (1½ sticks) unsalted butter, chilled and cut in slices
6 tablespoons shortening
⅓ cup ice water

For the topping:

¾ cup all-purpose flour
½ cup old-fashioned oats

½ cup light brown sugar, loosely packed

¼ teaspoon kosher salt

¼ cup melted unsalted butter

For the filling:

4 Granny Smith or other tart apples, cored, quartered,
    and sliced

4 Braeburn or other sweet apples, cored, quartered,
    and sliced

2 tablespoons sugar

2 tablespoons light brown sugar

1 tablespoon all-purpose flour

1 teaspoon ground cinnamon

¼ cup heavy cream

1 teaspoon vanilla extract

*To make the crust:* Place the flour, sugar, and salt in a food processor fitted with a steel blade and process until combined.
Add the butter and shortening, a little bit at a time, and process
until the mixture is pebbly. Gradually, while the machine is
running, add the water and process until the dough pulls away
from the sides and starts to form a ball. Form into two balls and
then press down to form two disks. Cover with a piece of parchment paper and refrigerate one disk at least 1 hour and up to

overnight. Cover the remaining disk with plastic wrap (over the parchment) and freeze up to 2 months for future use.

Preheat the oven to 425 degrees F.

*To prepare the topping:* Place the flour, oats, sugar, and salt in a bowl and toss well. Add the butter, mix until crumbly, and set aside.

*To make the filling:* Place the apples, sugars, flour, and cinnamon in a large bowl and toss well. Add the cream and vanilla and toss again.

Roll out the pie dough to form an 11- to 12-inch round and place in a 9-inch pie plate. Crimp the edges, if desired. Place the filling in the pie shell and transfer to the preheated oven. Bake for 15 minutes and then reduce the heat to 350 degrees F.

Remove the pie from the oven and cover with the topping, patting down so it adheres to the apples. Return to the oven and bake until lightly browned, about 1 hour to 1 hour 15 minutes.

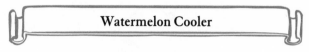

## Watermelon Cooler

Yield: 8 cups

3 cups cubed seeded watermelon

For the lemonade:

¾ cup sugar
1½ cups boiling water
4 cups cold water
2 cups freshly squeezed lemon juice
(about 8 lemons)
3 lemons, thinly sliced

*To make the frozen watermelon "ice"-cubes:* Place the watermelon in a blender or food processor fitted with a steel blade and process until blended. Transfer to 3 to 4 ice-cube trays and freeze.

*To make the lemonade:* Place the sugar and boiling water in a heatproof glass container and stir until the sugar has dissolved. Set aside to cool to room temperature. Cover and refrigerate overnight. Place in a large pitcher, add the cold water and lemon juice and stir well. Just prior to serving, add the lemon slices and some watermelon cubes to each glass.

# CHAPTER FIVE

# Potluck Pals

As Sylvia returned to the cupboards near the sink to take down glasses and wrap them carefully in paper before packing them in boxes, Anna steeled herself to search the cabinet where she had found the red-and-white gingham tablecloth for more mildewed linens. She hoped that Sylvia was correct and the damage had come about because her sister had not properly washed and dried the tablecloth before putting it away, and not because the windows or water pipes had leaked.

Kneeling, Anna reached deep into the cabinet and grasped another bundle of cloth—terry-cloth dish towels, she discovered when she brought them into the light, worn and suitable only for rags. She set them aside and felt around for more linens, but instead her fingers brushed something solid and smooth, and something else that felt like hard, twisted straw.

Tugging the objects into the light, she found that she held a glass oval serving dish cut with facets to gleam like crystal and a slightly larger woven basket with handles on the ends.

Taking one of the terry-cloth dish towels, she wiped a layer of dust from the cut-glass serving dish and held it up so the facets sparkled in the sunlight. Although it needed a good washing, not a single scratch or chip marred it, which suggested that it was either relatively new or that it had been cared for well as something precious and cherished. "Sylvia, look at this."

"More mildew?" As Sylvia leaned across the counter, her eyes widened at the sight of the dish and she let out a laugh of astonished delight. "My goodness, Anna, you've unearthed a treasure!"

Anna balanced the cut-glass dish on top of the woven basket and carefully rose. "The dish looks to be in perfect condition, but the basket—" Anna set them side-by-side on the counter so that she and Sylvia could examine them together. The tightly woven yellow straw was spotted black with mold, and one of the handles had unraveled and had come detached on one end. Only then did Anna notice how the basket was shaped to fit snugly around the cut-glass dish.

"My mother loved this set," Sylvia said, touching the plate lightly, tracing a diamond facet. "It was a wedding gift from a cousin, one of the few members of her family not to disown her after she eloped with my father."

"What?" Anna exclaimed.

"Oh, yes. Her parents wanted her to marry the son of a prominent New York businessman, but instead she ran off with a horse farmer from the middle of nowhere, Pennsylvania. All for love." Sylvia spoke the last phrase in a disdainful, bemused tone that Anna imagined was an imitation of the cold, unforgiving parents who had disowned their own child for following her heart. "My mother's cousin defied the entire family by sending this wedding gift."

Anna wasn't sure if sending the gift was as courageous as Sylvia seemed to think. Surely the cousin could have sent it secretly, so that only Sylvia's mother knew of her defiance. "I can tell your mother cherished it," she said instead. "The basket's a little damaged, but the dish is in perfect condition." Anna doubted Sylvia's mother would have approved of how they had been stored for the past few decades, but since that was Sylvia's sister's fault—and Sylvia's sister seemed to be a sensitive topic around Elm Creek Manor—she didn't mention it. "Did your mother save them for special occasions?"

"Yes and no," said Sylvia, smiling. "She used it on special occasions, but my mother always found a reason to call an ordinary day a special occasion, so the cut-glass dish was on our table quite often. And on other tables, as well." She placed the dish into the basket. "See how nicely it fits? The handles—before this one broke, of course—made it so easy to carry that my mother used this dish for every potluck dinner she attended. My father used to tease that she chose the recipe to fit the dish rather than choosing the right dish for a particular recipe."

"My mother did the same thing," said Anna. "But her favorite potluck carrier was a ceramic cake plate with a plastic cover and a handle." Anna had loved to attend potluck dinners in the neighborhood, sampling tasty casseroles and yummy desserts and matching them to their makers. She and her siblings had always compared notes afterward, evaluating the other ladies' cooking skills and declaring that their mom was the best cook of all.

"One of our campers told me a story once about a potluck birthday party she had celebrated as a child . . ." Sylvia rested her chin in her hand, thinking. "Yes, of course. Vinnie and the Potluck Pals."

"Vinnie?" The name sounded familiar. "Isn't she the camper we had that birthday party for back in August? What was it—her eighty-second or eighty-third birthday?"

"Something like that," Sylvia said. "If she wants to leave that detail a bit vague, I say we should let her. But she's shared other details with me and the Elm Creek Quilters, as well as many of our campers, so I'm sure she won't mind if I share them with you.

"You'd never know it from her sunny nature, but Vinnie had a tragic childhood. Her mother died when she was quite young, and her father simply fell apart. He could barely take care of himself, much less Vinnie and her elder brother. Vinnie began acting out in school—skipping classes, getting in fights—so she was sent to live with her aunt Lynn. Her aunt took good care of her, or so Vinnie says, but at the time she wanted nothing more than to go home to her father and brother.

"Her eighth birthday approached, but Vinnie had no interest in celebrating. Vinnie told her aunt that she wanted to spend her birthday with her father and brother or do nothing at all. Well, for reasons I don't know and probably wouldn't accept, her father didn't invite her to come home even for the day, so Vinnie resigned herself to no birthday party."

"His grief was probably too strong," said Anna.

"Perhaps." Sylvia shrugged dismissively as if to say that a stronger, better man would have risen to the occasion for his children's sake. Suddenly Anna remembered overhearing one of the Elm Creek Quilters mention that Sylvia's mother had died quite young, too. Perhaps Sylvia could not help but compare Vinnie's father to her own, a man who had apparently never disappointed his children.

"The morning of Vinnie's birthday arrived," Sylvia continued. "Her aunt and a friend woke her cheerfully and told her to
get up right away because the Potluck Pals were coming over
for her birthday party."

"The Potluck Pals?" Anna echoed, smiling. "Not Vinnie's
classmates, I'm guessing."

"No, the guests weren't Vinnie's circle of friends but
her aunt's, a group of ladies who met twice a month for a potluck meal and card games. The way Vinnie describes them—
shopgirls and secretaries and schoolteachers—they must
have been quite modern for their time, probably rather scan-
dalous."

"I like them already," said Anna.

"Oh, Vinnie, too. Vinnie adored them. On that day they
played cards and laughed and joked, and later they turned on
the radio and danced and danced. Vinnie told me it was the
first time since her mother had passed that she forgot her grief.
What an enormous burden to carry for such a little girl."

Anna nodded. It was so sad, but she couldn't help feeling
sorry for Vinnie's father, too. Surely he would have comforted
and consoled his daughter if he had been able.

But he had not, and Vinnie had been fortunate indeed to
have Aunt Lynn and the Potluck Pals.

"On that day, Vinnie says, she vowed always to celebrate
her birthday as happily as she could, to show gratitude for an-

other year despite the hardships it had brought along with its joys." Sylvia looked off into the distance, so wistful that Anna was tempted to ask if she were remembering lonely birthdays of her own, birthdays when she could have used a friend like Vinnie to remind her to count her blessings. But before she could bring herself to ask, Sylvia left her reverie and said, "Some years it's more difficult to truly celebrate, but Vinnie always found a way. That's what brought her to Elm Creek Manor."

"What do you mean?"

"After her husband died, she almost broke her promise to herself, but then at the last minute she came across a brochure for Elm Creek Quilt Camp and decided to spend her birthday with us. She thought it would distract her thoughts and keep her busy, and she didn't think she would feel her husband's absence so keenly surrounded by cheerful, busy quilters. When we heard about her circumstances, we surprised her on the morning of her birthday with a breakfast blueberry muffin with a birthday candle. All the campers sang to her, and I wish I had taken a picture because the expression on her face was priceless."

"That's why you had me serve everyone blueberry muffins that morning in August," Anna said, suddenly remembering. "It was a tribute to Vinnie's first birthday celebration at Elm Creek Manor."

Sylvia nodded. "Vinnie has promised to celebrate every birthday with us for as long as she can travel, and she's so spry and optimistic that I expect we will be contriving new ways to surprise her for years to come."

Anna agreed, thinking of the Potluck Pals and how they had brought much more than tasty dishes and birthday greetings to that lonely, grieving girl so long ago. She wished that for Vinnie's next surprise party—the surprise party that all the campers had come to expect though they never knew what form it would take—she could re-create that potluck party from so long ago. What better way to express her admiration for Vinnie's determination to create her own happiness despite her grief, for her resolve to find something worth celebrating in life, for her refusal to let loss turn her bitter and mistrustful?

Elm Creek Manor had so many stories, Anna thought, so many campers with tales as compelling as Vinnie's, and she longed to know them all. Each new story showed her a new facet of Elm Creek Quilts she had never suspected, like turning the cut-glass dish over in her hands near the sunny kitchen window and discovering new patterns of light cast upon the hardwood floor.

## Tomato Mushroom Ragout

Yield: sauce for 1 pound of pasta

1 tablespoon olive oil

1 Spanish onion, chopped

3 garlic cloves, minced

1½ pounds button mushrooms, wiped clean and sliced or
    chopped, stems included

1 teaspoon dried rosemary

½ ounce dried porcini mushrooms, chopped

One 28-ounce can whole tomatoes, including juice

¼ cup red wine

½ teaspoon kosher salt

Place a large skillet over medium-high heat and when it is hot, add the oil. Add the onion, garlic, mushrooms, and rosemary and cook until the vegetables have softened, about 10 minutes. Add the porcini, tomatoes, wine, and salt and cook until the ingredients come together, 20 to 30 minutes.

## Spinach Lasagna

Serves 6 to 8

1 pound whole or skim-milk ricotta cheese

2 large eggs

1 cup grated Parmesan cheese

1 large bunch flat-leaf spinach, chopped and blanched

One 8-ounce box no-cook lasagna noodles

1 pound Fontina or mozzarella cheese, thinly sliced or grated,
   or a combination of both

2½ cups tomato sauce

Preheat the oven to 350 degrees F. Lightly grease an 9 x 13-inch pan with olive oil.

Place the ricotta, eggs, and ½ cup Parmesan cheese in a medium-size mixing bowl and stir to combine. Add the spinach and gently mix.

*To assemble the lasagna:* Put three noodles across the prepared pan. Add one-third of the ricotta-spinach mixture, in dollops, on top of the noodles. Sprinkle with one-third of the Fontina cheese and then top with about ¾ cup tomato sauce. Repeat twice and then add another layer of noodles, another of sauce, another layer of Fontina cheese, and finish with the remaining Parmesan cheese.

Cover with aluminum foil, press down to tighten the layers and transfer to the oven. (If storing, cover with plastic wrap instead of foil. You can refrigerate up to 3 days or freeze up to 2 months.)

Bake for 30 minutes, remove the foil, and bake until the sauce is bubbling and the top is lightly browned, 25 to 30 minutes. Set aside to cool for about 10 minutes. Serve immediately or cover and refrigerate up to 3 days.

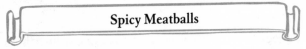

### Spicy Meatballs

Yield: 18 large meatballs

¼ cup panko bread crumbs
¼ cup all-purpose flour
1 teaspoon kosher salt
½ teaspoon black pepper
1 slice white bread
¼ cup whole milk
1 to 1¼ pounds ground beef
1 large egg, beaten

¼ cup finely grated Parmesan cheese

2 tablespoons finely chopped onion

Grated zest of ½ lemon

¼ cup chopped fresh Italian flat-leaf parsley leaves

1 teaspoon dried basil

1 teaspoon dried oregano

1 teaspoon crushed red pepper flakes

2 tablespoons olive oil

Place the bread crumbs, flour, salt, and pepper on a plate and mix well.

Place the bread and milk in a 4-quart bowl and set aside for 5 minutes.

Squeeze the milk out of the bread, discarding the milk. Using your hands, break the now mushy bread into small pieces. Add the ground beef and mix until the ingredients are well combined.

Using the back of your fist, create a crater in the middle of the meat mixture. Add the egg, cheese, onion, grated lemon zest, parsley, basil, oregano, and pepper flakes and combine until the mixture is well blended. When you think it's done, mix for another minute or two.

*To make the meatballs:* Using four fingers, take a piece of the meat mixture big enough to fill the palm of your hand, slightly larger than a golf ball. Press your hands together and start to roll the mixture by gently putting some pressure in the middle. It should form a slightly flat meatball 2 inches across. Dredge all sides of the meatballs in the panko mixture.

Have ready a large paper-towel-lined plate. Place a 10- to 12-inch skillet over medium heat and when it is hot, add the olive oil. Place as many meatballs in the pan as you can without crowding them. Sauté until deeply browned on all sides, about 8 minutes in all. Remove the meatballs from the pan with a slotted spatula and place on the prepared plate to drain. Serve immediately.

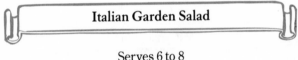

## Italian Garden Salad

Serves 6 to 8

For the dressing:

¼ cup fresh lemon juice

½ cup extra-virgin olive oil

1 small garlic clove, minced

¼ teaspoon kosher salt

½ teaspoon anchovy paste

For the salad:

1 bunch arugula, torn
1 bunch frisée, torn
1 head endive, chopped
1 small head radicchio, chopped
1 cup fresh basil leaves, torn

*To make the dressing:* Place the ingredients in a small bowl and whisk to combine. Cover and refrigerate up to 1 week.

*To make the salad:* Place the ingredients in a large salad bowl, add 3 to 4 tablespoons of the dressing, and gently mix. Serve immediately.

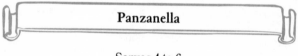

### Panzanella

Serves 4 to 6

2 cups cubed day-old Italian or French bread
2 medium tomatoes, diced
1 English cucumber, halved and thinly sliced
1 red onion, halved and diced
1 red, orange, or yellow bell pepper, diced
¼ cup coarsely chopped fresh basil leaves
1 tablespoon finely chopped fresh oregano leaves

½ cup coarsely chopped fresh Italian flat-leaf parsley leaves

2 garlic cloves, finely chopped or put through a press

1 tablespoon red wine vinegar

1 teaspoon kosher salt

½ teaspoon black pepper

2 tablespoons extra-virgin olive oil

Place the bread, vegetables, and herbs in a large mixing bowl.

Place the garlic, vinegar, salt, pepper, and oil in a bowl and mix well. Drizzle over the vegetables, cover, and refrigerate at least 1 hour and up to 4 hours.

## Olive Bread

Yield: 2 large rounds

1⅔ cups warm water

1 package active dry yeast (0.25 ounces = 2¼ teaspoons)

1 tablespoon sugar

1 tablespoon kosher salt

2 tablespoons olive oil

3¼ cups all-purpose flour

½ cup graham or whole-wheat flour

2 tablespoons cornmeal

2 teaspoons finely chopped fresh rosemary leaves

1½ cups very coarsely chopped green or black olives

Place the water, yeast, sugar, salt, and oil in a mixer fitted with a dough hook. While the mixer is running, add the flours. Knead on low speed until the dough starts to come together and then increase the speed until it is firm and smooth, 8 to 10 minutes in all.

Line two baking sheets with parchment or wax paper. Sprinkle with cornmeal.

Divide the dough into 2 pieces, shape into balls, and transfer to the baking sheets. Press the balls down and line each with half the rosemary and half the olives. Re-form the balls into loaf shapes, pressing the olives into the dough. Cover with damp towels and set aside until the loaves have doubled in size, about 2 hours.

Preheat the oven to 400 degrees F.

Transfer the baking sheets to the oven and bake until golden brown, about 25 minutes.

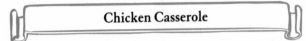

## Chicken Casserole

### Serves 4

7 to 8 bone-in skin-on chicken thighs, trimmed of fat and dried
    with a paper towel
1 teaspoon kosher salt
½ teaspoon black pepper
½ pound button mushrooms, wiped clean and sliced
1 small head fennel, chopped
2 carrots, chopped
2 celery stalks, chopped
1 Spanish onion, chopped
3 garlic cloves, thinly sliced
1 teaspoon dried thyme
1 teaspoon fennel seeds
2 cups dry white wine
2 cups chicken broth

¼ cup chopped fresh Italian flat-leaf parsley, for garnish

Sprinkle the chicken with the salt and pepper. Place a skillet over medium-high heat and when it is hot, add the thighs, skin side down, and sear until well browned, about 4 minutes per side. Using tongs, remove the chicken, and set aside on a plate.

Pour off all but 1 tablespoon of the fat. Reduce the heat to low, add the mushrooms, fresh fennel, carrots, celery, onion, garlic, thyme, and fennel seeds and cook until the vegetables are soft and golden, 10 to 15 minutes. Add the wine and chicken broth, return the chicken to the skillet, raise the heat to medium high and bring to a low boil. Cook, turning the chicken halfway, until the meat falls away from the bone, about 1 hour.

Cool, then skim off and discard the fat. Cover and refrigerate overnight. Reheat by placing over medium heat and cooking until warmed throughout, about 10 minutes. Serve garnished with the parsley.

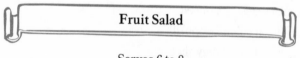

### Fruit Salad

Serves 6 to 8

1½ cups cantaloupe, cut with a melon baller

1 cup honeydew melon, cut with a melon baller

1 cup seedless green grapes

1 cup hulled fresh strawberries

1 cup fresh blueberries

1 cup diced fresh pineapple

1 cup fresh raspberries

1 banana, thinly sliced

¼ cup fresh mint leaves, left whole

Place all the ingredients in a bowl, toss, and serve immediately.

## Sour Cream Cake

Serves 10 to 12

1 cup whole milk

¾ cup poppy seeds

½ cup sour cream or whole-milk yogurt

1 tablespoon vanilla extract

2 tablespoons fresh lemon juice

1 cup (2 sticks) unsalted butter, at room temperature

1⅓ cups sugar

3 large eggs, at room temperature

2 cups all-purpose flour

1 tablespoon baking powder

½ teaspoon kosher salt

Preheat the oven to 350 degrees F. Lightly butter a standard Bundt pan.

Place the milk and poppy seeds in a small saucepan and bring to a low boil over medium-high heat. Set aside to cool for 15 minutes. Add the sour cream, vanilla, and lemon juice and mix well.

Place the butter and sugar in the bowl of a mixer fitted with a paddle and beat until light, fluffy, and a pale lemon color, 3 to 5 minutes. Add the eggs one at time, beating well and scraping down the sides of the bowl before each addition. Add 1 cup of flour and beat well. Scrape down the sides of the bowl and add half the reserved poppy seed mixture, continuing to beat.

Scrape down the sides of the bowl, add the baking powder, salt, and the remaining 1 cup of flour and beat well. Scrape down the sides of the bowl again, then add the remaining half of the poppy-seed mixture and mix well. Scrape down the sides of the bowl and pour into the prepared pan.

Transfer to the oven and bake until the top is just golden and a knife inserted comes out clean, 45 to 50 minutes.

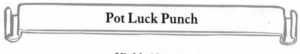

**Pot Luck Punch**

Yield: 12 cups

4 cups grapefruit juice

4 cups orange or tangerine juice

2 cups pomegranate juice

2 cups cranberry juice

Pour into a pitcher, stir well, and refrigerate up to 5 days.

# CHAPTER SIX

# Harvest Dance

 Sylvia washed the cut-glass dish and took it to the parlor for safekeeping, unwilling to risk damaging it in the carton with the other glassware or, worse yet, misplacing it in the discard box. When she returned to the kitchen, Anna had finished emptying the cabinet—towels and washcloths that went straight into the trash—and had moved on to the next. It was stuffed full of plastic storage containers, bottoms and lids arranged in no discernable pattern.

"Potlucks were once very popular around here," Sylvia remarked as she returned to the kitchen with another stack of brown paper for wrapping glassware. "The older generations sometimes called them 'covered-dish suppers,' but they've always been a part of the social life in the Elm Creek Valley."

Anna began sorting the plastic containers and lids into

piles, determined to recycle any pieces that didn't have a match. "It sounds like your mother enjoyed potlucks."

"Not just my mother, but all her friends and neighbors going back generations." Sylvia examined a dusty champagne flute for flaws, nodded her approval when it passed inspection, and wrapped it carefully in paper. "My Great-Great-Aunt Gerda wrote about an event in Creek's Crossing called the Harvest Dance."

"Where's Creek's Crossing?" asked Anna.

"Just down the road," Sylvia said with a teasing smile, then explained, "That was the original name for the town of Waterford, before the Civil War. The annual Harvest Dance was the highlight of their social season. In her memoir Gerda wrote about—oh, I believe it was two such occasions, one in 1857 and another a year later. In mid-November, after the work of the harvest was complete and before winter set in, families from throughout the valley would celebrate with a dance and covered-dish supper in town. Each lady wore her finest dress and brought her tastiest recipe to be sampled and evaluated by nearly everyone of her acquaintance. In addition to the feasting, there was music and dancing for hours and hours. I daresay the ladies were evaluated on the dance floor as well, since the Harvest Dance offered excellent opportunities for courtship."

Anna sat cross-legged on the floor, her work momentarily forgotten. "How did Gerda measure up?"

Sylvia shrugged and placed the wrapped champagne flute in a small box marked "Fragile" in bold letters. "By her own account, she was an excellent cook and only crumbs remained of any dish she brought to any gathering. Her sister-in-law—my great-grandmother—was a gifted seamstress, so I'm sure Gerda's dress passed muster as well. However, she was not an elegant dancer by her own admission, and she was plain and rather unlucky in love. Even so, she recorded her memories of those Harvest Dances in great detail, so they clearly made quite an impression on her, even if she didn't win a young man's heart on the dance floor."

Anna imagined the wives and mothers of the Elm Creek Valley coming in horse-drawn wagons with baskets of food to share, the farmers' bounty seasoned with the flavors of autumn, waiting eagerly or apprehensively to see how their efforts compared to their neighbors'. Recipes were surely exchanged as readily as compliments, just as quilt patterns were passed along from friend to friend at a quilting bee. Long-time rivals would keep a watchful eye on the serving tables to see whose recipe received the most returns for seconds, while young girls would wait anxiously to see if a favorite young man enjoyed her shoofly pie or chose another girl's spice cake. And after the dancing and celebration had ended, how proud each cook would have been to take home an empty dish at the end of the night, evidence that their recipe had won over the crowd—

and how chagrined to take home a pan still half full of a recipe that had failed to impress.

If she had been one of those farm women of long ago, Anna would have prepared her roast duck with raspberry coulis, or if that would have been showing off, she would have made pumpkin soup or German potato salad. As for a dancing partner, she hadn't dated anyone since breaking up with her last boyfriend several months before. If Summer were still away at graduate school, maybe Anna could ask Jeremy to go, just as friends, of course.

Anna smothered a laugh. Sylvia's story was so vivid that Anna could easily imagine herself in the midst of a celebration that probably was no longer observed. Unless . . . "Waterford doesn't still hold these Harvest Dances, right? I think I would have heard of them."

"No, the tradition faded out in the 1940s. So many young men were off fighting in the war that it seemed pointless to have a dance, and with the rationing of staples such as sugar and flour, the women of the Elm Creek Valley had enough trouble putting a decent meal on the table for their own families." Sylvia rested against the counter, her gaze far away. "But every autumn until then, we Bergstroms enjoyed the Harvest Dances tremendously. I remember my mother preparing bratwurst with apples and onions at the contraption that preceded this one—" She gestured to the old oven, shaking her head in disbelief at the thought that it had once been considered an upgrade. "She tried to follow Gerda's recipe precisely to win the approval of her in-laws, but my father interrupted her every few minutes to dance her around the kitchen. She laughed and protested that he must leave her alone or she would burn the food and become the laughingstock of the Elm Creek Valley, but my father declared that no one would dream of laughing at her, so light and graceful she was on the dance floor, so adored by all who knew her."

When Sylvia's expression became wistful, Anna said, "It sounds like your parents loved each other very much."

"They did, indeed." Sylvia shook off her reverie, smiled at Anna, and returned to her work. "Most people dream all their lives of finding such a love, but only the fortunate few find it. My parents sowed love in each other's hearts, and joy was their bountiful harvest, a harvest they shared with all who knew them. Thus their happiness was multiplied a hundredfold."

Anna watched Sylvia smiling to herself as she worked, and it occurred to her that she had missed the point of the Harvest Dance, a point that Sylvia's parents had understood implicitly. Naturally, Anna had focused on the competitive element of the event first, for as a professional chef she had a particular incentive to bring the tastiest dish to any friendly gathering. She suspected that unlike her, Sylvia's mother and most of the other women who had attended the Harvest Dances of years past had been happy simply to share the bounty of the family's farm with their friends and neighbors, to celebrate the work of the season now behind them, and to come together one last time before long nights and winter storms kept them indoors and apart from their beloved friends.

The Harvest Dance had brought them together for a joyous night of sharing and celebration, with music, laughter, love, and the flavors of autumn filling their hearts with sustenance for the long winter to come.

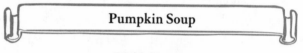

## Pumpkin Soup

Yield: 10 cups

1 tablespoon unsalted butter

1 Spanish onion, chopped

1 carrot, chopped

1 celery stalk, chopped

1 tablespoon chopped gingerroot

2 pounds fresh pumpkin, peeled, seeded, and diced
   (about 5 to 6 cups)

6 cups chicken broth

½ cup orange juice

½ cup heavy cream
1 tablespoon maple syrup

Place a 4-quart soup pot over medium-high heat and when it is hot, add the butter. Add the onion, carrot, celery, and ginger-root and cook until they have softened, about 10 minutes. Add the pumpkin and chicken broth and bring to a gentle boil. Reduce the heat to low and cook until the pumpkin is tender, about 40 minutes. Transfer the solids, in small batches, to a blender and process until smooth; gradually stir in the liquid, orange juice, cream, and maple syrup and serve immediately, or cover and refrigerate in a storage container up to 2 days.

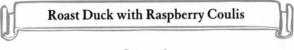

### Roast Duck with Raspberry Coulis

Serves 6

1 whole duck (about 7 pounds), excess fat and skin removed
    from neck and cavity
Kosher salt and black pepper
¼ cup molasses
Juice and rinds from 2 oranges
3 garlic cloves, minced

For the raspberry coulis:

12 ounces fresh or frozen raspberries
    (if frozen, thawed and drained)
¼ cup sugar
1 tablespoon molasses
1 tablespoon brandy

Preheat the oven to 250 degrees.

Using a sharp knife, carefully score the breast of the duck, about four times on each side, cutting through the skin to allow the fat to render. Season generously with salt and pepper.

Place the molasses, orange juice, and garlic in a small bowl and stir to combine. Place the orange rinds inside the cavity of the duck. Place the duck in a small roasting pan or large oven-proof skillet and brush with about one-quarter of the molasses mixture.

Transfer the duck to the oven and roast, basting every hour with the molasses mixture, until very tender and the legs move easily in their joints, about 4 to 5 hours.

*Prepare the coulis:* While the duck is cooking, place the raspberries, sugar, molasses, and brandy in a blender or food processor and process until smooth. Press the mixture through a fine-mesh strainer. Refrigerate until ready to use.

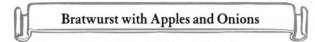

## Bratwurst with Apples and Onions

Serves 4 to 6

4 tablespoons vegetable oil

8 raw bratwurst

1 large onion, sliced thin

2 medium apples, peeled, cored, and cut into eighths

2 tablespoons unsalted butter

1 tablespoon all-purpose flour

½ teaspoon caraway seeds

One 12-ounce bottle lager beer

Kosher salt and black pepper, to taste

Place a large skillet over medium-high heat and when it is hot, add 2 tablespoons oil. Add the bratwurst and cook until browned on all sides but not quite cooked through, 5 to 7 minutes. Transfer the bratwurst to a plate.

Reheat the skillet to medium high, and when it is hot, add the remaining 2 tablespoons oil. Add the onion and cook until browned and beginning to soften, 3 to 5 minutes. Add the apples and cook until browned on all sides, about 2 minutes. Add the butter and when it has melted, add the flour. Stir to combine. Add the browned bratwurst, caraway seeds, and beer. Bring to a boil, reduce the heat to low, and simmer until the bratwurst is cooked through and the sauce is thickened, about 5 minutes. Season to taste with salt and pepper. Serve immediately.

## Chestnut Dressing

Serves 8 to 10

¼ cup (½ stick) unsalted butter

1 Spanish onion, chopped

1 carrot, diced

2 celery stalks, diced

8 cups packaged herb stuffing, such as Pepperidge Farm

One 16-ounce jar chestnuts, chopped

½ cup chopped fresh Italian flat-leaf parsley

¼ cup vermouth

1 to 2 cups chicken broth

1 teaspoon kosher salt, or more to taste

½ teaspoon black pepper

Preheat the oven to 325 degrees F. Lightly butter a casserole dish.

Place the butter in a large skillet over medium heat and when it has melted, remove all but 1 tablespoon to a small bowl.

Set aside. Add the onion, carrot, and celery to the skillet and cook until the vegetables have softened, about 10 minutes. Off the heat, add the stuffing mix, chestnuts, parsley, vermouth, and enough broth to moisten the bread crumbs.

Mix the chestnut-stuffing mixture with the vegetables in the skillet. Transfer to the casserole and drizzle with the reserved butter. Place in the oven and bake until heated through, about 15 minutes.

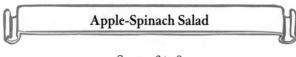

## Apple-Spinach Salad

Serves 6 to 8

For the dressing:

½ cup white wine vinegar
½ cup extra-virgin olive oil
1 teaspoon dry mustard
1 teaspoon kosher salt
¼ teaspoon Tabasco sauce

For the salad:

2 pounds flat-leaf spinach
2 large tart apples, cored and diced

½ cup dried cranberries

⅓ cup thinly sliced scallions

*To make the dressing:* Place the ingredients in a small bowl and whisk well.

*To make the salad:* Put the salad ingredients in a large bowl, add the dressing, and gently toss. Serve immediately.

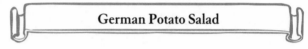

**German Potato Salad**

Serves 6 to 8

2 pounds small new potatoes, halved

¼ to ⅓ pound bacon

1 small red onion, chopped

3 tablespoons wine vinegar

3 tablespoons olive oil

2 teaspoons Dijon mustard

1 teaspoon kosher salt

½ teaspoon black pepper

¼ cup chopped fresh Italian flat-leaf parsley

2 tablespoons chopped fresh dill

Place the potatoes in a medium-size pot and cover with cold water. Bring to a boil over high heat and cook until tender, about 10 minutes (after the water boils). Drain and transfer to a large bowl.

Meanwhile, place the bacon in a large skillet and cook until the fat is rendered and the bacon is crisp, about 10 minutes. Transfer the bacon to a paper towel, crumble when cooled, and remove all but 2 tablespoons bacon fat from the pan. Reheat the pan and add the onion. Cook until tender and starting to brown, about 10 minutes. Add the vinegar, olive oil, mustard, salt, and pepper and whisk together. Pour over the still hot potatoes and very gently mix. Add the reserved bacon, parsley, and dill, toss gently, and serve immediately.

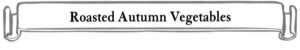

## Roasted Autumn Vegetables

Serves 6 to 8

2 red onions, sliced
4 red bell peppers, sliced
2 yellow bell peppers, sliced
2 yellow squash, sliced diagonally
2 tablespoons olive oil or vegetable oil

8 garlic cloves, chopped
2 teaspoons dried thyme
½ teaspoon kosher salt
½ teaspoon black pepper

Preheat the oven to 400 degrees.

Put all the ingredients together in a large bowl and toss well. Transfer to a baking pan. Transfer to the oven and roast until tender, about 50 minutes.

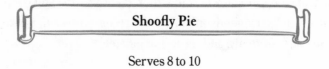

**Shoofly Pie**

Serves 8 to 10

For the crust:

1½ cups all-purpose flour
¼ teaspoon kosher salt
½ cup (1 stick) unsalted butter, chilled and cut in slices
¼ cup cold water

For the filling:

¾ cup all-purpose flour
½ cup light brown sugar, loosely packed

4 tablespoons (½ stick) unsalted butter, chilled and
    cut in slices
¾ cup molasses
2 large eggs
½ cup hot water
1 teaspoon baking soda
½ teaspoon ground cinnamon
¼ teaspoon ground cloves
¼ teaspoon kosher salt

*To make the crust:* Place the flour and salt in the bowl of a stand mixer fitted with a paddle. Add the butter and mix on medium speed until the mixture resembles coarse sand, about 1 minute. Add the water and mix until just combined and the dough comes together, less than 1 minute. Shape the dough into a disk, wrap in plastic wrap, and refrigerate about 1 hour.

Preheat the oven to 350 degrees.

Roll out the dough to ⅛-inch thickness on a lightly floured surface. Place the dough in a 9-inch pie tin and trim the overhang to 1 inch. Fold under the rim of dough and decoratively crimp. Cover and refrigerate while you prepare the filling.

*To make the filling:* Place the flour and brown sugar in a small bowl. Add the butter and mix with your fingers until the mixture resembles coarse meal. Place two-thirds of the mixture in the bottom of the piecrust.

Place the molasses, eggs, ½ cup hot water, baking soda, cinnamon, cloves, and salt in a large bowl and whisk until the mixture begins to foam. Pour the molasses mixture into the pie shell and top with the remaining flour mixture.

Transfer to the oven and bake until set, 35 to 40 minutes. Cool on a rack.

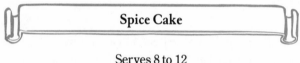

### Spice Cake

Serves 8 to 12

For the cake:

1 cup (2 sticks) unsalted butter, at room temperature

1½ cups light brown sugar, loosely packed

2 large eggs, at room temperature

1 cup buttermilk or full-fat yogurt

1 tablespoon grated lemon zest (1 lemon)

1 teaspoon vanilla extract

2 cups all-purpose flour

1 teaspoon baking soda

½ teaspoon kosher salt

½ teaspoon ground cinnamon

½ teaspoon ground nutmeg

½ teaspoon ground ginger

⅛ teaspoon black pepper

Pinch of ground cloves

1 cup toasted walnuts or pecans (measured whole),
    then finely ground (optional)

For the soaking syrup:

½ cup light brown sugar, loosely packed

¼ cup water

½ cup (1 stick) unsalted butter, melted

1 teaspoon vanilla extract

Pinch of kosher salt

Confectioners' sugar for garnish

Preheat the oven to 350 degrees F. Lightly butter and flour a 9-inch Bundt pan.

*To make the cake:* Place the butter and brown sugar in the bowl of a mixer fitted with a paddle and beat until well creamed, 3 to 5 minutes. Add the eggs and beat again.

Place the buttermilk, lemon zest, and vanilla in a bowl and beat well.

Place the dry ingredients in a bowl, toss to combine, and add, in three additions, to the butter mixture, alternating with the buttermilk mixture. Scrape down the sides of the bowl between additions. Add the nuts, if using, and mix again.

Place in the prepared pan, transfer to the oven, and bake until a tester comes out clean, 45 to 60 minutes.

*Prepare the soaking syrup:* While the cake is baking, place the ingredients in a small pot and bring to a boil over high heat for 2 minutes.

Cool the cake in the pan for 5 minutes, invert, and then prick the surface of the cake with a toothpick. *Brush* (don't pour) on the soaking syrup and cool to room temperature. Cover with plastic wrap and serve immediately or set aside for up to 2 days, turning it over every half day or so. Sprinkle with confectioners' sugar.

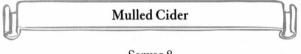

## Mulled Cider

Serves 8

½ gallon apple cider

¼ teaspoon ground allspice

½ teaspoon ground ginger or ground cardamom

2 cinnamon sticks

Strips of peel from 1 orange

½ cup to 1 cup Calvados, rum, or brandy

Place the cider, spices, cinnamon sticks, and orange peel strips in a large pot and bring to a boil over high heat. Reduce the heat to low and simmer for 10 to 15 minutes, depending upon how strong you want the cinnamon to be. Add 1 to 2 table-spoons Calvados to each cup and top with the hot cider.

# CHAPTER SEVEN

# Thanksgiving

 When Anna finished clearing out the last of the cabinets by the window, she rose, stretched, and brushed off the seat of her jeans, wondering what part of the enormous workload she should tackle next. Her thoughts lingered on Sylvia's story of the Harvest Dance, on the flavors of the season—pumpkins, squash, apples, roasted potatoes—and the importance of sharing one's blessings with friends and loved ones. The Bergstroms had apparently understood this well, and that spirit of sharing and gratitude infused Elm Creek Manor even into the present day, nurtured and strengthened by Sylvia and the Elm Creek Quilters.

"That's it for the champagne flutes," Sylvia said, closing the box. "I thought we had another dozen more but I suppose we must have broken a few through the years."

"We have lots of other cupboards to search," Anna said, gesturing to the cabinetry lining the walls on both sides of the stove and the refrigerator.

Sylvia eyed all those they had not yet emptied, hands on her hips. "That's encouraging in one regard and quite discouraging in another."

"We'll finish in time," Anna reassured her. "If we have to, we'll postpone the work a bit."

"And find ourselves rescheduled for February or March? Absolutely not. We'll clear out the kitchen on time even if it means throwing everything into boxes entirely at random and sorting it out later. I'd rather not operate in such haphazard fashion, but if it comes down to the wire . . ." Sylvia opened another cabinet, shaking her head. "I must stop distracting us from the task at hand. Less rambling and more work is the order of the day, I think."

"I enjoy your stories," Anna protested. "They don't distract me. They motivate me."

"I can't imagine why," scoffed Sylvia, reaching deep into a cupboard.

Anna couldn't bring herself to explain. The Elm Creek Quilters had a long, shared history—and Anna had a lot of catching up to do. Sylvia's stories helped her learn more about the manor and the people who had made it their home, past and present. The other Elm Creek Quilters might have heard these stories and others like them many times through the years, but it was all new to Anna. She would never feel like a true Elm Creek Quilter if she didn't understand the common history they took for granted.

"Oh, for goodness' sake." Sylvia withdrew something from the cupboard that at first glance reminded Anna of the basket carrier for the cut-glass dish. Then Sylvia blew off some dust and set it on the counter, and Anna saw that while it was indeed woven of straw, it was shaped like a curved cone and was far less finely crafted than the basket.

"My sister's handiwork," Sylvia said, studying it. "A seventh-grade art project. Strange, but it doesn't look as bad as I remember."

"What is it?" asked Anna tentatively, not wishing to offend.

Sylvia's eyebrows rose. "It's a cornucopia, of course."

"Oh, right, right." Once Anna knew what it was supposed to be, she was able to see the resemblance. "That's not bad for a seventh grader's work."

"You'd think it was David in marble the way my parents carried on about it when Claudia brought it home from school."

"You know how parents are," Anna said. "I bet they acted the same way about your schoolwork."

"That's a bet you would lose."

Anna couldn't believe it, but Sylvia spoke so adamantly

that she decided not to pursue the question. "So this cornucopia," she said instead, "I'm guessing it was for Thanksgiving?"

"That's right. While my classmates and I were tracing around our hands to make crayon-on-paper turkeys, my sister's class worked on these marvels." Sylvia sighed and shook her head as Anna picked up the cornucopia to examine it. "Their teacher was a bit eccentric. When I had her a few years later, she had us make papier-mâché pilgrims. Mine was so frightful it would have been better suited for Halloween."

Anna burst out laughing. "I'd love to see it. Please tell me it's in one of these cabinets."

"I certainly hope it was discarded long ago. In fact, if I recall correctly, I threw it in the trash myself before Thanksgiving weekend was over." Sylvia took the cornucopia, and for the first time Anna saw her regard it with something close to fondness. "This cornucopia was the centerpiece of our Thanksgiving table every year from the time Claudia brought it home from school. When we gathered for our holiday feast, each member of the family placed something in the cornucopia that represented what they were most thankful for that year. My mother always placed a photograph of our family, naturally. My father usually added something like an apple or a horseshoe to represent our thriving farm. Claudia usually drew a picture of our parents, or of Jesus, or sometimes our family with Jesus—a transparent attempt to win praise from the adults for her goodness and piety, if you ask me, but they always fell for it."

"What were you thankful for as a child?" Anna asked.

"Oh, when I was very young I would cram a favorite toy into the cornucopia and leave little room for anything else. In later years I would contribute a favorite poem, or a picture, and once I tried to re-create Elm Creek Manor in popsicle sticks. Claudia said it looked like an outhouse, but my father said it was an excellent likeness."

Anna nodded, hiding a smile, and didn't point out that Sylvia's father, at least, appeared as biased about his younger daughter's artistic achievements as his elder's.

"Grandparents and aunts and uncles and cousins all contributed something to the cornucopia," Sylvia continued, "and after supper, we examined the items one by one as each person explained what they were most grateful for that year and why."

"It sounds like a wonderful tradition."

"It was, indeed. Some years it wasn't easy to narrow our many choices to only one, and other times it was difficult to feel sincerely grateful for anything. Either way, our tradition never failed to remind us to consider how much we had to be grateful for, even in the most difficult of times."

Anna watched as Sylvia gently placed the cornucopia in a clean, sturdy carton. "Maybe we could resume the tradition this Thanksgiving."

"Perhaps we should," said Sylvia. "This year, I for one will need the reminder to count my blessings."

"Why?" asked Anna. "Is something wrong?"

Sylvia's expression softened and she reached across the counter to pat Anna's hand. "Nothing serious, my dear. It's just that it will be a lonelier Thanksgiving than usual around here this year. Usually the Elm Creek Quilters spend Thanksgiving Day with their families, of course, but the next day, we gather here for quilting and a special feast. Everyone brings a dish to pass—"

"Another potluck," Anna broke in, smiling.

Sylvia nodded. "We're partial to them, as you've already discovered. This potluck, however, has a theme: Our recipes have to use leftovers from our Thanksgiving dinners. Sarah makes a turkey tetrazzini that's second to none."

Anna still didn't understand the reason for Sylvia's sudden melancholy. "But not this year?"

"Unfortunately, no. Since Judy moved to Philadelphia, she obviously can't make it, and you've no doubt already overheard Gwen lamenting that Summer is too busy with her graduate school studies to come home until the end of fall quarter."

Anna had not heard any such thing, and Summer's boyfriend drove her to the manor almost every day. "Does Jeremy know?"

"I have no idea, dear. I assume Summer has told him."

Sylvia eyed Anna curiously. "But if he hasn't mentioned it, perhaps not."

Anna shrugged, suddenly uncomfortable, although she could not say exactly why. "Two people will be missing, but surely the rest of you can celebrate."

"Three. Bonnie's traveling, too, and I don't think she'll return to Waterford for Thanksgiving. If anything, she'll spend the holiday with one of her children out of town." Then Sylvia shook her head as if to clear it of nonsense. "What's the matter with me? I've been thinking only of the friends who have departed and not of the new friends recently arrived. That's reason enough to be grateful, to give thanks. You're absolutely right, Anna. We must continue our tradition, and—" She gave her sister's cornucopia an affectionate pat. "This will be our centerpiece. I already know what I'll tuck inside it on Thanksgiving Day. You'll come, won't you, Anna? I insist. For Thanksgiving as well as the Elm Creek Quilters' celebration the next day."

"I wouldn't miss it," Anna exclaimed, "but I'm not coming as a guest. Do you think I'd let anyone else prepare the first Thanksgiving feast in my new kitchen? I've had the menu planned for two weeks!"

She had already resolved that it would be the most delicious Thanksgiving dinner any of the Elm Creek Quilters had ever tasted. Now she had an extra incentive to make the occasion memorable, not for the absence of beloved friends, but for the enticing aromas and scrumptious flavors of roast turkey, butternut squash, sweet potatoes, and pumpkin pie—all the traditional flavors of the season presented as Anna's gift of gratitude to her new colleagues and future friends.

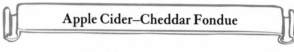

### Apple Cider–Cheddar Fondue

Serves 6

4 cups shredded sharp cheddar cheese

1 tablespoon plus 1 teaspoon cornstarch

1¼ cups apple cider

2 teaspoons lemon juice

⅛ teaspoon ground nutmeg

Kosher salt and black pepper

12 ounces cooked sausage, cut into bite-size pieces

1 small loaf sourdough bread, cut into cubes

2 large apples, cored and sliced

Place the cheese, cornstarch, cider, lemon juice, and nutmeg in a heavy-bottomed pot and cook over medium heat until the cheese has melted and the mixture is smooth, about 5 minutes.

Season to taste with salt and pepper. Transfer to a fondue pot and serve immediately with sausage, bread, and apples.

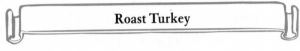

### Roast Turkey

Serves 10 to 12

One 12- to 15-pound turkey
2 medium onions, halved and coarsely chopped
2 to 3 carrots, coarsely chopped
2 celery talks coarsely chopped
1 lemon, quartered
2 rosemary branches, 4½ to 5½ inches, or thyme, 3 to 4 inches
4 tablespoons (½ stick) unsalted butter, melted
2 teaspoons kosher salt
1 teaspoon black pepper
1 cup water

Adjust one oven rack to the lowest position and remove the remaining racks. Preheat the oven to 425 degrees F and line the bottom of a 12-inch V-rack with aluminum foil. Poke holes in the foil with the tip of a skewer or knife. Place the V-rack in a large shallow roasting pan.

Remove the neck, heart, and gizzard and set aside to make

the gravy later. Discard the liver (the soft, reddish brown globelike thing).

Rinse the turkey, inside and out, several times with cold running water. Pat dry with a paper towel several times: The turkey skin should be as dry as possible.

Place the onions, carrots, celery, lemon, and rosemary in a medium bowl and toss to combine. Set aside. Brush the turkey breast with 2 tablespoons butter, then sprinkle with 1 teaspoon salt and ½ teaspoon black pepper. Set the turkey *breast side down* on the V-rack. Brush the turkey back with the remaining 2 tablespoons butter and sprinkle with the remaining 1 teaspoon salt and ½ teaspoon black pepper. Fill the cavity with half the vegetable mixture. Scatter the remaining mixture in the roasting pan; pour 1 cup water over the scattered vegetables.

Transfer the pan to the oven and cook for 1 hour. Remove the roasting pan from the oven and transfer it to a countertop; close the oven door. Do not place the turkey on the oven door.

Lower the oven temperature to 325 degrees F.

Using a clean dish towel or two pot holders, turn the turkey breast side up. Return the roasting pan to the oven and cook until the dark thigh meat reaches 170 to 180 degrees F, the legs move freely, and the juices run clear (not pinkish red), about an additional 2 hours. Remove from the oven and let rest, uncovered, for about 20 minutes. (Throw the dish towel in the washing machine.)

## Cranberry Corn Bread Dressing

### Serves 8 to 10

1 tablespoon olive oil or unsalted butter

1 Spanish onion, chopped

4 celery stalks, diced

2 Granny Smith apples, peeled if desired, and diced

1 cup fresh cranberries

7 to 8 cups day-old crumbled corn bread
   (homemade or store-bought)

½ cup chopped walnuts or pecans

3 tablespoons chopped fresh Italian flat-leaf parsley

2 teaspoons dried sage

3 tablespoons chopped fresh rosemary, or 1 tablespoon dried

3 tablespoons chopped fresh thyme, or 1 tablespoon dried

1 teaspoon kosher salt

2 tablespoons dry vermouth

2 large eggs

Preheat the oven to 350 degrees F. Lightly butter a 9 x 13-inch pan.

Place a medium-size skillet over low heat and when it is

hot, add the oil. Add the onion, celery, apples, and cranberries and cook until tender, 15 to 20 minutes.

Add the remaining ingredients, mix well, place in the prepared pan, and transfer to the oven. Bake until golden brown on top, about 35 minutes.

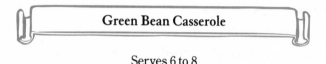

### Green Bean Casserole

Serves 6 to 8

1 tablespoon olive oil

1 tablespoon unsalted butter

2 pounds green beans, trimmed and blanched

Grated zest of ½ orange

½ teaspoon kosher salt

¼ teaspoon black pepper

Place a large skillet over high heat and when it is hot, add the oil and butter. When the butter has melted, add the green beans and cook until heated through, about 3 minutes. Add the orange zest, salt, and pepper.

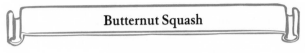

## Butternut Squash

Serves 6 to 8

2 medium-size butternut squash, cut in half lengthwise

¼ cup (½ stick) unsalted butter, at room temperature

2 tablespoons honey or maple syrup

Juice and grated zest of ½ lemon

1 teaspoon grated fresh gingerroot (optional)

½ teaspoon kosher salt

¼ teaspoon black pepper

Preheat the oven to 400 degrees F. Lightly butter a baking sheet. Place the squash, cut side down, on the prepared baking sheet and roast until tender, about 1 hour. Set aside to cool slightly. Scoop out the seeds and remove the skin.

Transfer the squash to a food processor fitted with a steel blade, add the remaining ingredients, and process until smooth. Cover and refrigerate overnight in a storage container or place in a large pot and cook until heated through. Serve immediately.

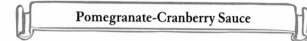

## Pomegranate-Cranberry Sauce

Yield: about 2 cups

One 12-ounce bag cranberries (3 cups)
¼ cup pomegranate or orange juice
½ cup light brown sugar, loosely packed
½ teaspoon kosher salt
Grated zest of 1 orange
¾ cup lightly toasted pecans or walnuts, coarsely chopped
Seeds from 1 large pomegranate

Place the cranberries, pomegranate juice, and brown sugar in a small saucepan and cook over medium-high heat, until the cranberries are soft and have absorbed all the liquid, about 10 minutes. Set aside to cool.

Add the salt, orange zest, nuts, and pomegranate seeds. Serve immediately or cover and refrigerate for up to 2 weeks.

## Sweet Potatoes

Serves 4 to 6

4 sweet potatoes, peeled and cut in thick rounds

½ cup sugar

½ cup water

4 tablespoons unsalted butter

¼ cup fresh lemon juice

½ teaspoon kosher salt

Preheat oven to 400 degrees F.

Place the sweet potatoes in an 8 x 8-inch pan. Place the sugar, water, butter, lemon juice, and salt in a small saucepan and bring to a boil over high heat. Pour the sugar syrup over the sweet potatoes, cover with foil, and bake for 30 minutes.

Remove the foil and pour off all the liquid into a bowl. Pour the liquid back over the sweet potatoes (basically basting them), return to the oven without the foil, and cook until caramelized and bubbly, about 30 additional minutes.

## Pumpkin Pie

Serves 8 to 10

### For the crust:

3 cups all-purpose flour

1 teaspoon sugar

¾ teaspoon kosher salt

¾ cup (1½ sticks) unsalted butter, chilled and cut in slices

6 tablespoons shortening

⅓ cup ice water

### For the filling:

3 large eggs

1 cup light brown sugar, loosely packed

2 cups canned pumpkin puree

1⅓ cups light cream

1 teaspoon ground ginger

1 teaspoon ground cinnamon

½ teaspoon kosher salt

½ teaspoon ground nutmeg

⅛ teaspoon ground cloves

Whipped cream, for garnish

*To make the crust:* Place the flour, sugar, and salt in a food processor fitted with a steel blade and process until combined. Add the butter and shortening, a little bit at a time, and process until it is pebbly. Gradually, while the machine is running, add the water and process until the dough pulls away from the sides and starts to form a ball. Form into two balls and then press down to form two disks. Cover with parchment paper and refrigerate one disk at least 1 hour and up to overnight. Cover the remaining disk with plastic wrap (over the parchment paper) and freeze for up to 2 months.

Preheat the oven to 400 degrees F.

Roll out the pie dough to form an 11- to 12-inch round and place in a 9-inch pie plate. Crimp the edges if desired. Poke holes with a fork in the bottom of the crust. Cover the shell with aluminum foil, transfer to the oven and bake for 10 minutes. Remove the foil and fold it into a strip so that you can use to cover the crust edge only. Return it to the oven and bake until the bottom is just golden, about 10 minutes.

*To make the filling:* Place the eggs and brown sugar in the bowl of a stand mixer fitted with a paddle or whisk and blend until smooth, about 1 minute. Add the remaining ingredients and pour into the prepared pie shell. Transfer to the oven and bake until firm, 25 to 30 minutes. Set aside to cool. Serve at room temperature or refrigerate at least 2 hours and serve cold, accompanied by whipped cream.

## Apple-Pear Crisp

Serves 6 to 8

For the filling:

3 cups diced Granny Smith apples

3 cups diced Bartlett pears

2 tablespoons sugar

2 tablespoons all-purpose flour

For the topping:

1 cup all-purpose flour

1 cup rolled oats

3 tablespoons sugar

¼ cup light brown sugar, loosely packed

½ teaspoon kosher salt

½ cup (1 stick) unsalted butter, melted

Preheat the oven to 375 degrees F.

*For the filling:* Place the fruit, sugar, and flour in a large bowl and toss well. Pour into an 8 x 8-inch pan.

*For the topping:* Place the flour, oats, sugars, and salt in a large mixing bowl and toss well. Add the butter and toss again until it forms a consistent texture. Sprinkle on top of the fruit.

Place the pan in the oven and cook until lightly browned on top, 35 to 40 minutes. Serve warm or at room temperature.

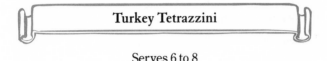

**Turkey Tetrazzini**

Serves 6 to 8

For the filling:

2 tablespoons unsalted butter

2 Spanish onions, chopped

1 carrot, cut in small dice

1 celery stalk, cut in small dice

10 to 12 ounces button mushrooms, sliced

2 tablespoons all-purpose flour

3½ cups turkey or chicken broth

½ cup heavy cream

3 tablespoons dry sherry

Juice and grated zest of 1 small lemon

½ teaspoon dried thyme

2 teaspoons kosher salt

1 teaspoon black pepper

4 cups shredded turkey or chicken

4 cups cooked spaghetti, cut in half

2 cups frozen peas

For the topping:

½ cup panko breadcrumbs

½ cup finely grated Parmesan cheese

1 teaspoon kosher salt

Preheat the oven to 450 degrees F.

*To make the filling:* Place a large ovenproof skillet over medium-high heat and when it is hot, add the butter. Add the onions, carrot, celery, and mushrooms and cook until the onions have softened and are just turning golden, about 10 minutes. Slowly, stirring well, add the flour and cook until it is fully incorporated. Slowly, stirring all the while, add the stock a tablespoon at a time, and cook until the mixture has thickened, about 4 minutes. Off heat, add the cream, sherry, lemon juice, zest, thyme, salt, and pepper and stir well. Add the turkey, spaghetti, and peas and stir well.

*For the topping:* Place the panko, Parmesan cheese, and salt in a small bowl and mix to combine. Sprinkle over the filling.

Transfer to the oven and cook until golden, about 20 minutes. Serve immediately.

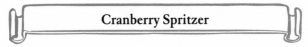

## Cranberry Spritzer

Yield: 8 cups

4 cups cranberry juice
4 cups seltzer
1 lemon, sliced
1 lime, sliced

Place all the ingredients in a large pitcher and serve immediately.

# CHAPTER EIGHT

# Christmas

 For the rest of the morning, Anna and Sylvia worked steadily and briskly, spurred on by the approaching deadline and the amount of work that yet remained. Despite Anna's protests that she enjoyed Sylvia's stories, Sylvia, lost in her own thoughts, shared no more tales from the manor's past.

By noon they had made good progress—and had worked up an appetite. Anna offered to cook them a hot lunch, but Sylvia insisted that Anna was already working hard enough and sandwiches would suit her just fine. So Anna scrounged for cold cuts and condiments while Sylvia sliced a loaf of bread, and before long they were sitting with their backs against the wall with paper plates balanced on their laps, munching sandwiches and complimenting each other on the work they had already accomplished.

"Our efforts will be well worth it," Sylvia promised, "when you're cooking up a storm in your dream kitchen."

Anna didn't doubt that for a moment, but state-of-the-art appliances and cabinetry didn't make a kitchen the heart of a home. When the workmen had finished and all the pots and pans and dishes had been transferred from cartons to well-organized cupboards, one problem would remain: how to make the spirit of Elm Creek Quilts and the history of the Bergstrom family apparent to everyone who crossed the threshold.

After lunch, they resumed their work with renewed energy, chatting about the new kitchen layout, the convenience of the center island and improved pantry shelving, and the luxury of nearly doubling the square footage by knocking out the wall to the adjacent room. "The manor doesn't lack for pleasant places to sew," Sylvia said when Anna asked her if she would miss her sitting room. "What we need is a larger kitchen."

And a more welcoming kitchen, Anna added silently, wishing she could think of a way to make it so.

They had been steadily filling cartons and dragging them into the banquet hall out of the way for more than an hour when Sylvia suddenly cried out, "Great-Aunt Lydia's aprons! I can't believe they've been tucked away here all this time."

Anna abandoned her work and hurried over to see the latest newly discovered treasure. Sylvia had climbed to the top of a four-step foldable ladder to reach a cabinet above the refrigerator and was holding on to the safety bar with one hand while groping into the cabinet with the other.

"Here, let me do that," Anna said, alarmed by the older woman's precarious balance.

"Nonsense, dear, I'm fine," Sylvia insisted, but then relented. "Oh, very well. You are a bit taller."

They traded places. Anna reached deep within the cabinet and withdrew a stack of neatly folded cotton prints—florals, fruits, novelties, mostly small-scale designs in a rainbow of pastels. Anna handed the stack to Sylvia, who eagerly draped each apron across the counter as Anna hopped down from the ladder and joined her in admiring the collection. There were fourteen different aprons, similar in size but varying in style and embellishments, with no two fabrics the same. Some covered only the skirt while others also covered the blouse; several had large pockets on the front, while others boasted lace trim and others were tailored to show off a trim hourglass figure. Judging by the faded fabric, loosening seams, and occasional stains and burns, all had been used often.

Sylvia tied a daisy-print apron around her waist and turned around to model it for Anna. "It's hard to believe such pretty things began as feed sacks, isn't it?"

Anna fingered a lace-trimmed apron made from a print of ripe red cherries on a yellow-and-white check background. "Feed sacks?"

"Oh, yes. When I was a girl—and even when my grand-mother was a girl—feed for farm animals as well as flour and other kitchen staples were sold in cotton sacks. Farming families were much too frugal to waste perfectly good fabric, so we washed the empty sacks and stitched them into clothing. My great-aunt Lydia had a penchant for pretty aprons, as you can see, which she indulged with what she considered 'free' fabric."

"She made enough for the whole family," Anna remarked. "Even a family as large as yours."

"True, she did, but if my great-aunt loved a particular fabric, she made sure the apron fit her and her alone so that she wouldn't have to share it and it would last longer," Sylvia handed one of the slender, tailored aprons to Anna, who held it up to her more ample figure, shook her head, and returned it. "Lydia thought she had the other women of the family fooled, but they knew what she was up to. She was such a delightful person otherwise that her sister, my great-aunt Lucinda, convinced the others to indulge her in this one vanity."

"Lucinda must have been a very tolerant sister," Anna said, knowing that her own sisters never would have allowed her to get away with something like that.

"She was, indeed." Sylvia rested her hand upon another, more generously sized apron sewn from a holly leaf print on a red background. "It helped, I think, that Lydia made Lucinda this special apron from a holiday fabric that she particularly admired. Why don't you try it on?"

Anna obliged, and Sylvia's face lit up with satisfaction upon discovering that it fit Anna as well as if it had been made especially for her. "It suits you," Sylvia declared, looking her over. "The red fabric complements your dark hair and coloring. Lucinda looked pretty in it, but I think it looks even better on you."

"It was Lucinda's favorite?" Anna asked, embarrassed by the praise.

"Oh, yes, but she wore it only during the Christmas season, which for us began on December 6 with St. Nicholas Day." Sylvia's gaze grew far away, and Anna knew she was imagining the kitchen as it had appeared long ago, when her great-aunts had filled it with the enticing aromas of a Christmas feast. "All the women of my family were fine cooks, but Lucinda was an especially skilled baker. She made all the traditional German Christmas cookies we children loved so much—*Anisplätzchen, Lebkuchen*, and *Zimsterne*—and, of course, she joined in when all the women of the family made apple strudel."

"I bet that was quite a production," said Anna, who had made traditional apple strudel in culinary school. It remained one of her favorite memories of her student years—chatting with friends while they peeled apples, confiding similar dreams to run their own restaurants someday, debating how much of which spices created the most "Christmasy" flavor, and laughing over their first attempts to stretch the dough.

"Gerda's apple strudel was legendary in the Elm Creek Valley," Sylvia said, "and although the succeeding generations followed her recipe to the last pinch of salt, no Bergstrom woman could equal her in the kitchen. It was our tradition to make many strudels each year, one for the family to enjoy at breakfast on Christmas Day and others to give to friends. Unfortunately, the tradition died out with my generation. My sister and I tried to make strudel after our mother passed away, but you know how women of that time cooked—they rarely wrote anything down, and rarely used standard measurements."

Anna nodded. "They measured by handfuls and pinches, not cups and teaspoons. My grandmother still cooks that way. I had to watch her very carefully while she cooked, or I never would have learned the secrets to her tomato sauce and pasta."

"It's a shame when those old recipes fade from family memory." Sylvia sighed, untied her great-aunt's apron, and placed it on the counter with the others. "What I wouldn't do for a taste of apple strudel the way my mother made it, or a bite of *Lebkuchen* fresh from Lucinda's Santa Claus cookie jar. So many of my fondest Christmas memories bring me back to this kitchen, warm and festive and fragrant with cinnamon and gingerbread. Those, to me, are the flavors of Christmas."

"I know exactly what you mean," said Anna.

She untied the apron and was about to place it with the others when Sylvia held up a hand to stop her. "No, dear, it's yours. Perhaps you'll indulge me by wearing it this Christmas as you prepare your own special holiday dishes."

Touched, Anna nodded and folded the apron carefully. "I will. Thank you."

But she had already decided to indulge Sylvia in a way that she hoped would please her even more. This Christmas, she would treat Sylvia to all of her favorite holiday flavors, from the Christmas cookies of her childhood to the traditional German *Jägerschnitzel* for Christmas dinner, and a hot cup of cocoa with a slice of apple strudel for dessert.

Anna had a feeling the legendary Gerda Bergstrom would approve.

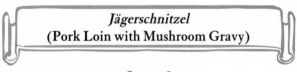

### *Jägerschnitzel*
### (Pork Loin with Mushroom Gravy)

Serves 6

8 thin pork cutlets, pounded to ⅛-inch thickness
    (just over 1 pound)
1 teaspoon kosher salt
½ teaspoon black pepper

2 large eggs, beaten

1½ cups panko breadcrumbs

4 to 6 tablespoons vegetable oil

4 slices bacon, finely chopped

1 medium onion, finely chopped

1 pound button mushrooms, sliced

2 tablespoons unsalted butter

1 tablespoon all-purpose flour

2 cups chicken broth

2 tablespoons sour cream

1 teaspoon finely chopped fresh thyme

1 tablespoon finely chopped fresh parsley

Preheat the oven to 200 degrees. Have 2 paper-towel-lined plates ready.

Sprinkle the pork cutlets with the salt and pepper.

Place the eggs in a shallow bowl. Place the bread crumbs on a plate.

Dip the cutlets in the beaten egg and then in the bread crumbs to coat evenly.

Place a large skillet over medium heat and when it is hot, add 2 tablespoons of oil. Add the cutlets, in batches, and cook until evenly browned, about 2 minutes per side, adding oil as necessary. Place on one of the prepared plates to drain, then transfer to the oven to keep warm while you prepare the sauce.

Place the bacon in a large skillet over medium heat and cook until the fat is rendered and the bacon is crisp, 5 to 7 minutes. Remove the bacon with a slotted spoon to a paper-towel-lined plate to drain. Raise the heat to high, add the onion, and cook until browned, 3 to 5 minutes. Add the mushrooms and butter and continue cooking until the mushrooms are soft and brown, about 10 additional minutes. Add the flour and stir to combine. Add the chicken broth and cook until reduced and thickened, about 5 minutes. Off the heat, add the sour cream and herbs and stir to combine. Serve immediately over the pork cutlets.

## Cornish Game Hens

Serves 8

Four 1-pound Cornish game hens, rinsed with cold water
     several times and patted dry with paper towels
1½ teaspoons kosher salt
½ to 1 teaspoon black pepper
1 tablespoon unsalted butter
Juice of 1 small lemon

Preheat the oven to 400 degrees F.
     Remove the backbones and press the hens down flat.

Transfer to a wire rack placed in a large roasting pan and sprinkle with the salt and pepper. Dot with the butter and pierce in several places with a sharp knife. Roast until the juices run clear and the hens have browned, about 25 minutes. Turn on the broiler and broil until deeply browned, 3 to 5 minutes. Add the lemon juice to the pan juices and drizzle over the hens. Serve immediately.

**Mushroom Medley**

Serves 6 to 8

2 tablespoons olive oil

1 pound button mushrooms, wiped clean

1 pound assorted wild mushrooms, wiped clean and trimmed

2 garlic cloves, minced

1 teaspoon chopped fresh rosemary leaves

1 teaspoon kosher salt

½ teaspoon black pepper

Preheat the oven to 400 degrees F.

Place all the ingredients in a bowl and mix well. Transfer the mushrooms, in a single layer, to a baking sheet, place in the oven, and roast until they are lightly browned and have released their juices, about 20 minutes. Serve immediately.

## Sage and Thyme Potatoes

Serves 6 to 8

3 pounds new potatoes, halved or quartered

2 tablespoons olive oil

4 to 6 garlic cloves, finely chopped

1 tablespoon fresh thyme leaves or 1 teaspoon dried,
    plus additional fresh thyme, for garnish

1½ teaspoons kosher salt

½ teaspoon dried sage

Preheat the oven to 450 degrees F.

Place the potatoes in a large bowl. Add the olive oil, garlic, thyme, salt, and sage and mix until combined. Spread the mixture on a baking sheet or in a large baking pan and roast until browned, 35 to 45 minutes. Serve immediately, sprinkled with thyme.

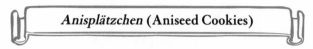

### *Anisplätzchen* (Aniseed Cookies)

Yield: 18 cookies

1½ cups all-purpose flour
½ teaspoon baking powder
1½ teaspoons ground anise seeds
3 large eggs
1 cup sugar
½ teaspoon grated lemon zest

Lightly butter a large baking sheet.

Place the flour, baking powder, and anise seeds in a medium bowl. Place the eggs, sugar, and lemon zest in the bowl of a stand mixer fitted with a whisk and mix on high speed until light and fluffy, 3 minutes. Slowly, while the mixer is running, add the flour mixture and mix on low speed until combined, about 30 seconds. Drop by teaspoonfuls on the prepared baking sheet, 1 inch apart. Let stand, uncovered, overnight at room temperature.

Preheat the oven to 350 degrees F.

Place the baking sheet in the oven and bake until the cookies puff and are beginning to brown, 10 to 15 minutes. Transfer to a wire rack to cool.

## *Lebkuchen*
## (Gingerbread Cookies with Almonds)

Yield: 3 dozen cookies

1½ cups sliced or slivered almonds, ground until very fine
2½ cups all-purpose flour
1 teaspoon baking powder
½ teaspoon kosher salt
2 teaspoons ground cinnamon
1 teaspoon ground ginger
½ teaspoon ground cloves
½ teaspoon ground nutmeg
¾ cup honey
¾ cup light brown sugar, loosely packed
½ cup (1 stick) unsalted butter, at room temperature
2 large eggs
8 ounces (1⅓ to 1½ cups) mixed candied fruit
2 cups confectioners' sugar
3 tablespoons water
Candied cherries, for garnish (optional)

Preheat the oven to 350 degrees F. Grease three baking sheets.
Place the almonds, flour, baking powder, salt, and spices in

a bowl and mix to combine. Place honey, brown sugar, and butter in the bowl of a stand mixer fitted with a paddle and mix on high speed until smooth, about 30 seconds. Add the eggs one at a time, and mix until combined. Slowly add the flour mixture and mix until just combined. Add the candied fruit and mix until evenly distributed.

Using a small cookie scoop or your hands, shape the dough into 2-inch balls and place 2 inches apart on the baking sheets. Using the bottom of a greased glass or measuring cup, gently flatten the balls to ½-inch-thick disks. Transfer to the oven and bake until the edges are browned, 12 to 14 minutes. Transfer to a wire rack to cool.

Place confectioners' sugar and water in a small bowl and stir until smooth. Spread the icing evenly over the cookies. Garnish with candied cherries, if desired. Air-dry.

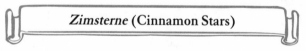

## *Zimsterne* (Cinnamon Stars)

Yield: 2 dozen cookies

3 cups sliced almonds
1 teaspoon ground cinnamon
1 teaspoon grated lemon zest

2 cups confectioners' sugar, plus extra for rolling

3 large egg whites

Preheat the oven to 350 degrees F.

Place the almonds, cinnamon, and lemon zest in the bowl of a food processor fitted with a steel blade and process until finely ground. Add 1 cup confectioners' sugar and process until combined.

Place the egg whites in the bowl of a stand mixer fitted with a whisk and beat on high speed until they hold stiff peaks, about 1 minute. Slowly add the remaining cup of confectioners' sugar and continue mixing on high speed until thick and creamy, about 2 minutes longer. Set aside ⅔ cup of this meringue mixture for glazing the cookies.

Add the almond mixture to the remaining meringue and mix on low speed to combine.

Lay out a sheet of parchment or wax paper and sprinkle generously with confectioners' sugar. Place the dough on the paper and pat into a flat circle. Sprinkle with more confectioners' sugar and top with a second piece of the parchment paper. Roll out the dough to ¼-inch thickness. Use a star-shaped cookie cutter to cut out the cookies and arrange on a greased baking sheet. Repeat with the remaining scraps.

Transfer to the oven and bake until golden brown and set, about 10 minutes. Spread the tops of the cookies with the reserved meringue and bake until the glaze just begins to color, about 5 minutes longer. Cool on a rack.

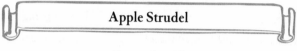

### Apple Strudel

Serves 8 to 10

If you can only find small sheets of phyllo (9 x 14 inches), simply divide the apples and make two small strudels, each using five sheets of phyllo.

3 large assorted apples, like Macintosh and Golden Delicious, peeled, cored, and thinly sliced (about 3 heaping cups)
½ cup raisins
¼ cup plain toasted breadcrumbs
¼ cup light brown sugar, loosely packed
¼ cup chopped walnuts
¼ teaspoon ground cinnamon
¼ teaspoon kosher salt
1 teaspoon lemon juice
5 large sheets phyllo dough (14 x 18 inches)
5 tablespoons unsalted butter, melted

1 teaspoon sugar

1 tablespoon confectioners' sugar

Preheat the oven to 475 degrees F. Lightly butter a baking sheet.

Place the apples, raisins, breadcrumbs, brown sugar, walnuts, cinnamon, salt, and lemon juice in a medium bowl and toss to coat evenly.

Lay out one sheet of phyllo dough and brush with butter. Top with a second sheet of phyllo dough and brush with butter. Repeat with the remaining phyllo and butter, creating a stack of five sheets of phyllo and ending with butter. (You will have a little bit of butter remaining.)

Arrange the apples in a strip about one-third up from the bottom, leaving about 2 inches on either end. Lift the bottom of the phyllo over the top of the apples. Fold in the sides, and continue to roll up the apples tightly.

Place the strudel, seam side down, on the prepared baking sheet. Brush the top with the remaining butter and sprinkle with granulated sugar. Transfer to the oven and bake until golden brown, about 15 minutes. Cool to room temperature. Sprinkle with confectioners' sugar before serving.

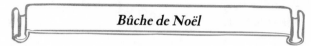

### Bûche de Noël

Serves 8 to 10

For the cake:

⅔ cup all-purpose flour

⅓ cup unsweetened cocoa powder

1 teaspoon baking powder

6 large eggs

¾ cup sugar

1 teaspoon vanilla extract

For the filling and frosting:

1¼ cups (2½ sticks) unsalted butter, softened

3 cups confectioners' sugar

2 tablespoons milk

4 ounces semisweet chocolate, melted

½ teaspoon vanilla extract

2 tablespoons instant coffee powder

*To make the cake:* Preheat the oven to 350 degrees F. Grease an 11 x 17-inch jelly-roll pan, line with parchment paper or aluminum foil, and grease and flour the paper.

Place the flour, cocoa powder, and baking powder in a medium bowl and mix to combine.

Place the eggs, sugar, and vanilla in the bowl of a stand mixer fitted with a whisk and mix on high speed until pale and fluffy, 3 minutes. Reduce the speed to low and slowly add the flour mixture. Mix until just combined.

Pour the batter into the prepared jelly-roll pan, taking care to spread the batter into all corners of the pan. Bake until the surface springs back when poked with your finger and a toothpick inserted in the center of the cake comes out clean, 15 to 20 minutes. Run a knife along the perimeter of the pan and immediately turn the cake out onto a rack covered with a clean dish towel. Set aside to cool while you prepare the buttercream.

*To make the filling and frosting:* Place the butter in the bowl of a stand mixer fitted with a paddle and mix on high speed until fluffy. Reduce the speed to low and slowly add the confectioners' sugar, mixing until just combined. Remove half of the buttercream and set aside.

Add 1 tablespoon milk, the melted chocolate, and vanilla to the remaining buttercream and mix to combine. Transfer to a bowl, cover, and refrigerate. Place the remaining 1 tablespoon of milk in the microwave for 10 to 15 seconds until warm and stir in instant coffee until dissolved.

Return the remaining buttercream to the mixing bowl. Add the coffee mixture and mix until just combined.

Place the cake on the dish towel on a hard surface (like the counter) and trim ¼ inch from each side of the cake (the edges tend to be dry).

Arrange the cake so that a long side is directly in front of you. Spread the coffee buttercream in an even layer over the cake, going right up to the edges on three sides—the long side directly in front of you and the two short sides—but only to within 1 inch of the top. Gently roll the cake, using the dish towel to lift and your fingers to tuck the edge. Roll the cake completely, ending with the seam side down. Use the dish towel to help press the cake into an even roll. Remove the dish towel and refrigerate the cake, covered, at least 1 hour.

Place the roulade on a serving plate and frost with the chocolate buttercream; reserve about ½ cup for touch-ups. Cut off a 3-inch piece from one end at a 45-degree angle. Cut off a thin slice from the other end so it is at the same angle; eat or discard the thin slice. Attach the 3-inch piece, flat side down, on top of the roulade in the center. Press down slightly to adhere it to the cake. Using the reserved buttercream, frost the empty side of the "stump" on top of the "log." Using a fork, gently trace lines in the buttercream so that it resembles a log.

Cover and refrigerate at least 1 hour and up to 2 days.

## Christmas Cocoa

Yield: about 8 cups

½ cup unsweetened cocoa powder

⅓ cup sugar, or more if desired

2 cups heavy cream

6 cups whole milk

1 tablespoon vanilla extract

Candy canes, for stirring

Place the cocoa powder, sugar, and cream in a saucepan and cook, whisking, over low heat and until the cocoa has been incorporated. Slowly add the milk and vanilla and heat until warmed throughout, whisking all the while. Serve immediately in heated cups, garnished with candy canes.

# CHAPTER NINE

# Happy New Year

 Anna hung the Christmas apron in the hall closet and helped Sylvia pack the others in a box already half-full of placemats and napkin rings. She wasn't sure what Sylvia intended to do with her great-aunt Lydia's collection, but she could tell from the older woman's expression that she was conflicted. The aprons had been worn past their usefulness, and yet they held too much sentimental value to be thrown away.

Anna carried the box into the banquet hall and placed it on the floor alongside the others, wondering if the aprons really belonged among the items they intended to store in the new cabinets. But where else would Sylvia put them? In the attic with the scores of other possessions Bergstroms of generations past had been unable to part with? No, the aprons belonged in the kitchen, but it would be a shame to hide them in a high cupboard, out of sight and out of mind once again.

When Anna returned to the kitchen, she found Sylvia tugging hard on the handle to a drawer that would not budge. "It's jammed," Sylvia said, exasperated, as Anna came over to help. "I tried to push the obstruction aside with a spatula, but I couldn't find whatever's wedged the drawer shut."

"Maybe it caught on something and it slipped underneath." Anna found the spatula on the counter and knelt down to peer beneath the drawer. Sure enough, a dark shape blocked the right-hand glide, but a few taps of the spatula moved it out of the way. Anna pulled out the entire drawer and set it on the floor as Sylvia reached inside and removed what appeared at first glance to be a small stack of paper.

As Sylvia shuffled through the pieces, each about the size of an index card, her eyes widened in amazement. "Oh, my goodness. This is Lucinda's handwriting."

All at once, Anna knew what Sylvia had discovered. "Old family recipes?"

"It certainly appears so. Look here." Triumphant, Sylvia held up a single card. "*Feuerzangenbowle*. Red wine, lemon, orange, cinnamon, allspice, cardamom—oh, I can smell the citrus and spices even now. I can see my father stirring the kettle over the fire, the steam rising, our guests gathering around eagerly waiting for a sip."

"You'll have to translate for me," said Anna, taking the card Sylvia held out to her.

"*Feuerzangenbowle* literally means 'fire tongs punch,' " Sylvia explained. "It's a traditional German beverage my family served on New Year's Eve. As the ingredients brewed over the fire, my father would soak a *Zuckerhut*—that's a cone of sugar, but, of course, a chef would know that—in rum, set it afire, and let the caramelized sugar drip into the punch." Sylvia eagerly read the next card. "*Pfannkuchen*. Pork roasted with apples. Sauerkraut." She quickly skimmed through the rest of the cards. "I can't believe it. All of our family's favorite traditional New Year's dishes." She shook her head, perplexed. "But why these recipes, out of all our family favorites?"

"Maybe Lucinda made a New Year's resolution to abandon the family tradition of not writing down recipes," Anna suggested, smiling. "Or maybe she assumed everyone would remember how to make the everyday meals, but would forget those you served only once a year."

"Perhaps, but then again—" Sylvia removed her glasses, gazed thoughtfully at the dilapidated stove for a moment, and put her glasses on again. "We ate pork with apples as well as sauerkraut throughout the year. We made a point to eat them on New Year's Day, of course, for good luck, but we did eat them at other times."

"Pork and sauerkraut were considered good luck?" Anna asked. "I would have been in for a rough year, then. I'm not a big fan of sauerkraut."

"Only because you haven't tried the Bergstrom family recipe." Smiling, Sylvia flourished a yellowed card covered on both sides with backward slanted handwriting. Lucinda had apparently been a leftie. "If you sat down to dinner with us on New Year's Day, we would have teased and cajoled you into taking at least a tiny bite. Germans consider pigs to be good luck, Lucinda always told us children, because a farm family who had a pig to feed them through the long, cold winter was fortunate indeed. Cabbage leaves represented money, so a meal of pork and sauerkraut on New Year's Day would guarantee good fortune throughout the coming year."

"Guarantee, you think?"

"Well, perhaps not guarantee, but it couldn't hurt." Sylvia flipped through the cards once more, shaking her head as if she still couldn't believe her eyes. "Ah. Lentil soup. My sister and I loved the hint of oregano and red wine."

"Eating lentils on New Year's Day is an Italian tradition," said Anna, surprised that a family so passionate about its German heritage had shared the custom. "My grandmother insisted that eating lentils would ensure good luck and prosperity throughout the New Year."

"Naturally," said Sylvia. "Since lentils are round, like coins, eating them will obviously bring one riches in the coming year."

"Obviously," Anna agreed wryly. "Now if only someone

would invent a food shaped like a winning lottery ticket. And another shaped like world peace."

"If only it were that easy." Sylvia fell silent as she read each card in turn. She seemed to be savoring her great-aunt's handwriting as if the written words were as flavorful as the dishes they described. Then she sighed, arranged the cards in a neat pile, and set them on the counter. "I always feel such a curious play of emotions at the turning of the year. We celebrate and hope and anticipate, of course, as we look forward to a fresh start, a new beginning, and we resolve to improve ourselves and change for the better. At the same time, I've always sensed a small undercurrent of apprehension, because none of us knows for certain what the New Year will bring."

"That might account for all the superstitions about luck in the New Year," Anna said. "We eat particular foods or observe certain rites to help ward off bad luck and bring good fortune." She gestured to the recipe cards. "Maybe that's why your great-aunt finally wrote down these recipes. Maybe she wanted to pass along some good luck to her descendants."

"Not Lucinda. She wasn't the slightest bit superstitious. My grandmother Elizabeth was the one who never met a superstition she didn't embrace." Sylvia smiled at the memory. "No, I suspect Lucinda wanted to preserve our family recipes so that her nieces and nephews could one day re-create the flavors of our childhood and thus always remember how joyfully our family welcomed the New Year. That's how the New Year should begin—with happiness and celebration, affection and good cheer, so we may move into the future with courage and hope, knowing that love will sustain us through whatever comes."

And now, thanks to the foresight of Great-Aunt Lucinda, Sylvia could re-create those cherished New Year's dishes of celebrations long past. Or, Anna thought, a friend who loved to cook could create them for her.

When Sylvia's back was turned, Anna tucked the cards carefully into a box of silverware so they would not be misplaced again. Come New Year's Eve, she would need them.

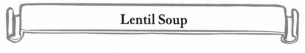

### Lentil Soup

Yield: 10 to 12 cups

1 cup brown lentils, picked over and rinsed

1 carrot, peeled and sliced

2 celery stalks, including leaves, sliced

1 small red onion, chopped

1 teaspoon dried Greek oregano

¼ cup barley

10 to 12 cups low-sodium chicken, beef, or vegetable broth

One 14.5-ounce can whole peeled tomatoes, coarsely chopped

¼ cup dry red wine

Kosher salt and black pepper

Lemon quarters, for garnish

Fresh Italian flat-leaf parsley or basil leaves, for garnish

Place the lentils, carrot, celery, onion, oregano, barley and broth in a heavy-bottomed saucepot or stockpot and bring to a boil over high heat.

Lower the heat and simmer, uncovered, until the soup has thickened and reduced by about one-quarter, about 2 hours.

Add the tomatoes and wine, stir, and continue cooking for 1 to 2 hours. Add salt and pepper to taste.

Transfer to a container, cover and refrigerate at least overnight and up to 3 days.

Place in a pot and gently reheat. Garnish with lemon wedges and fresh herbs.

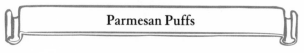

## Parmesan Puffs

Serves 6 to 8

½ cup (1 stick) unsalted butter, at room temperature

1 cup all-purpose flour

1 cup grated Parmesan cheese

½ teaspoon kosher salt

Place all the ingredients in a food processor and pulse until it forms a dough. Transfer the dough onto a piece of parchment paper and form it into a log about 2 inches in diameter. Wrap in the parchment and then in plastic. Refrigerate at least 2 hours and up to 1 week.

Preheat the oven to 325 degrees F. Lightly butter a baking sheet.

Cut the log into ¼-inch-thick rounds. Place them about 1-inch apart on the baking sheet and bake for 10 minutes. Raise the heat to 500 degrees and bake until they are golden brown, about 5 additional minutes.

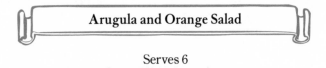

## Arugula and Orange Salad

Serves 6

For the dressing:

2 tablespoons grated Parmesan cheese

¼ cup olive oil

¼ cup balsamic vinegar

For the salad:

2 bunches arugula, torn

1 head romaine, torn into bite-size pieces

2 celery stalks, peeled and thinly sliced

1 orange, peeled, sectioned, and seeded, then diced

*To make the dressing:* Place the Parmesan, olive oil, and balsamic vinegar in a small bowl and whisk to combine.

*To make the salad:* Place the arugula, romaine, celery, and orange in a serving bowl and drizzle with the dressing. Serve immediately.

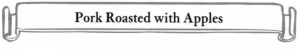

**Pork Roasted with Apples**

Serves 6

For the brine:

¼ cup boiling water

2 tablespoons kosher salt

1½ to 2 cups apple cider

1 tablespoon coarsely ground black pepper

1 sprig fresh rosemary

1 bay leaf

1 teaspoon fennel seeds

2 garlic cloves, minced

1 pork loin, 2 to 2½ pounds, tied by your butcher

For the apples:

2 tablespoons unsalted butter

2 large onions, halved and then sliced

1 fennel, quartered, cored, and then sliced

2 large apples, peeled, cored, quartered, and then sliced

1 teaspoon dried thyme

1 cup apple cider

Up to ½ cup water

Kosher salt

2 tablespoons olive oil

*To make the brine:* Place the salt and water in a large bowl and mix until the salt has dissolved. Add the remaining ingredients, including the pork, then cover and refrigerate at least 1 day and up to 3. Remove the pork and wrap it in paper towels—to dry it out. Refrigerate until ready to use.

*To make the apples:* Place the butter in a large skillet over medium-high heat and when it has melted, add the onions. Cook until they start to brown a bit, about 10 minutes. Add the fennel, apples, and thyme and cook until they just start to color and soften, about 10 minutes. Add the cider, then cover and cook until the mixture thickens and is completely softened, about 10 minutes. If it dries out too much, add up to ½ cup water.

Preheat the oven to 400 degrees F.

*To cook the pork:* Sprinkle generously with the salt. Place a large skillet over medium-high heat and when it is hot, add the oil. Add the pork and cook until well browned on all sides, about 8 minutes. Transfer to the oven and cook until the internal temperature reaches 150 degrees F. Set aside for 10 minutes and then serve, with the apples on the side.

### Sauerkraut

Serves 8

2 pounds sauerkraut, rinsed and drained

12 ounces lager-style beer

1 cup chicken broth

¼ cup light brown sugar, loosely packed

¾ teaspoon caraway seeds

Kosher salt and black pepper

Place all the ingredients in a medium saucepan and bring to a boil over medium-high heat. Reduce the heat to low and simmer 30 minutes. Season to taste with salt and pepper.

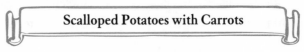

## Scalloped Potatoes with Carrots

Serves 6 to 8

¾ cup heavy cream

¾ cup whole milk

1 teaspoon kosher salt

1 garlic clove, minced

Pinch of black pepper

Pinch of ground nutmeg

1¾ to 2 pounds new potatoes, cut in ⅛-inch slices

2 carrots, cut in ⅛-inch slices

¼ cup freshly grated Parmesan cheese

Preheat the oven to 350 degrees F. Lightly butter a gratin dish or an 8 x 8-inch pan.

Place the cream, milk, salt, garlic, pepper, and nutmeg in a small saucepan and bring to a low boil. Reduce the heat to low and cook until slightly thickened, 3 to 5 minutes. Place the potatoes and carrots in the buttered dish and pour the hot cream over them. Press down with the back of a spoon.

Transfer to the oven and bake until the potatoes and carrots are tender, 45 to 55 minutes. Raise the heat to 425 degrees F, press the potatoes down and sprinkle with the Parmesan cheese.

Continue baking until golden brown, about 15 minutes. Serve immediately.

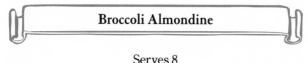

## Broccoli Almondine

Serves 8

1 tablespoon unsalted butter
½ cup sliced or chopped almonds
2 broccoli heads, florets chopped and blanched,
   stems discarded (or saved for another use)
1 to 2 tablespoons fresh lemon juice
¼ teaspoon kosher salt
Pinch black pepper

Place a large skillet over medium-high heat and add the butter. When the butter has melted, add the almonds and broccoli, and cook until the almonds are lightly toasted and the broccoli is heated through, about 5 minutes. Add the lemon juice, salt, and pepper. Serve immediately.

## *Pfannkuchen*

Serves 6 to 8

For the apples:

¼ cup (½ stick) unsalted butter, at room temperature
4 Granny Smith apples, peeled, cored, and thinly sliced
¼ cup light brown sugar

For the batter:

6 large eggs
1 cup whole milk
1 teaspoon vanilla extract
1 cup all-purpose flour
½ teaspoon kosher salt
Confectioners' sugar, for garnish

Preheat the oven to 450 degrees.

*To prepare the apples:* Place two 10- to 12-inch skillets over medium heat and to each, add half the butter. When the butter has melted, add half the apples and brown sugar to each and cook until golden, 15 to 20 minutes. Do not stir often.

*To prepare the batter:* Place the eggs, milk, and vanilla extract in a large bowl and mix well. Add the flour and salt and stir until smooth.

Pour half the batter over the cooked apples in each skillet and transfer the skillets to the oven. Bake until the pancakes have puffed up and are golden brown, about 15 minutes. Serve immediately, garnished with confectioners' sugar, from the skillets.

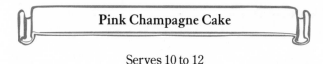

## Pink Champagne Cake

Serves 10 to 12

For the cake:

2½ cups all-purpose flour

1 tablespoon baking powder

1 teaspoon kosher salt

¾ cup (1½ sticks) unsalted butter, at room temperature

1½ cups sugar

6 large egg whites

1 cup Champagne or sparkling wine

For the coconut filling:

4 tablespoons unsalted butter

2 cups marshmallows (about 16 large marshmallows)

1 cup flaked coconut

For the pink frosting:

1¼ cups (2½ sticks) unsalted butter, softened

3 cups confectioners' sugar

2 tablespoons Champagne or sparkling wine

¼ teaspoon red food coloring

½ teaspoon kosher salt

Preheat the oven to 350 degrees. Grease and flour two 9-inch cake pans.

*To make the cake:* Place the flour, baking powder, and salt in a medium bowl and stir to combine. Place the butter and sugar in the bowl of a stand mixer fitted with a paddle and mix until light and fluffy, about 1 minute. Add the egg whites and mix on high speed until light and airy, about 1 minute. Add half the dry ingredients and mix until combined. Add the Champagne and mix until combined. Add remaining dry ingredients and mix until just combined. Mix an additional 30 seconds on high speed. Pour the batter into the prepared pans and bake until a toothpick inserted in the center of the cake comes out clean, 20 to 25 minutes. Cool in the pans 10 minutes, then remove and cool on a rack to room temperature.

*To prepare the filling:* While the cakes are cooling, place the butter and marshmallows in a medium-size pot over medium heat and cook, stirring often, until melted and smooth. Add the coconut and stir to combine. Set aside to cool to room temperature.

*To prepare the frosting:* Once the cakes are cool, place the butter in the bowl of a stand mixer fitted with a paddle, and mix on high speed until light and fluffy, about 30 seconds. Add the confectioners' sugar 1 cup at a time, and mix until combined. Add the Champagne, red food coloring, and salt and mix on high speed until frosting is smooth and fluffy, about 30 seconds.

*To assemble the cake:* Place one layer of the cake on a cake plate or stand. Top with the coconut filling and spread in an even layer. Top with the remaining cake layer, top side down, and frost with the pink frosting.

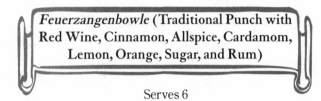

*Feuerzangenbowle* (Traditional Punch with Red Wine, Cinnamon, Allspice, Cardamom, Lemon, Orange, Sugar, and Rum)

Serves 6

½ cup sugar

1 cup dark rum

1 750 ml bottle red wine

2 cinnamon sticks

⅛ teaspoon cardamom

6 allspice berries

Peel of 1 orange (without the white pith)

Peel of 1 lemon (without the white pith)

Place the sugar and the rum in a heavy-bottomed saucepan and very carefully light the rum. Let the flames burn until the sugar begins to caramelize, about 30 seconds. Cover the pot to extinguish the flame. When the flame is out, carefully add the wine, spices, and fruit peels. Set the pot over medium heat and cook until hot but not boiling, about 2 minutes. Serve immediately.

# CHAPTER TEN

# Farewell Breakfast

Sylvia and Anna worked through the afternoon, occasionally chatting, sometimes lost in their own thoughts. Within the drawers and cupboards they discovered other long-forgotten treasures—potholders Claudia had woven at Girl Scout camp, a small bowl and spoon that had once belonged to Sylvia's younger brother—cherished keepsakes that told Anna how significant a setting the kitchen had been in the history of the Bergstrom family. She was determined to preserve that history, for regardless of the changes she was bringing to the appearance and the function of the kitchen, its spirit must remain the same.

She resolved to do it, somehow.

In the late afternoon they broke for supper—sandwiches and a can of soup Anna reluctantly heated in the microwave, wishing she had thought to bring something more palatable from home—and afterward worked on until evening. Then, fatigued but proud of the work they had accomplished, they agreed to call it a day and reunite in the morning to finish the job.

Anna offered to prepare blueberry muffins and a yummy cranberry-orange coffee cake at her apartment and bring them for breakfast, if Sylvia would put on a large pot of coffee to share. Sylvia agreed, adding, "It will be our own Farewell Breakfast, bidding good-bye to the old kitchen as we look forward to a fresh start in the new one."

"We can eat on the cornerstone patio if you like," Anna said, picking up on Sylvia's allusion to a favorite Elm Creek Quilts celebration. On Saturday mornings during camp season, the Elm Creek Quilters served their guests a delicious al fresco breakfast buffet on a broad, square patio paved with the same gray stones from which the manor had been built. Lilac bushes surrounded the patio, leafy, green, and lush, loveliest in spring when their fragrant blossoms bloomed. Hidden among the tree branches, where the patio touched the northeast corner of the manor, was the cornerstone that Sylvia's great-grandfather Hans Bergstrom had placed with the help of his wife, Anneke, and his sister, Gerda, the legendary cook. Anna had felt an unexpected thrill the first time she read the proud engraving, BERGSTROM 1858, and realized that from that day forward she too would contribute to the rich history of Elm Creek Manor.

"It may be a bit too brisk to have breakfast outdoors," Sylvia said, gazing out the window at the autumn sky, darkening with the close of day. A few bare limbs etched stark lines through the colorful foliage, signs of the certainty of winter. "And what's a Farewell Breakfast without show-and-tell? Our campers love showing off their handiwork and sharing their favorite memories of their week at quilt camp."

"We've enjoyed a show-and-tell all day long," Anna reminded her. "Your red-and-white picnic tablecloth, your sister's cornucopia, your great-aunt Lydia's apron collection—and we're only two-thirds of the way through the cabinets. I can only imagine what we'll discover tomorrow."

"More keepsakes, more memories," Sylvia promised. "As well as more things that should have been thrown out long ago. Sometimes I wish my ancestors had been more discerning about what they kept and what they threw away."

"But aren't you glad they weren't?" Anna protested. "What if someone had thrown out the basket for your mother's cut-glass dish because the handle broke? You might not have shared its story with me. And what if someone had decided that your great-aunt's aprons were too worn and fit only for rags? I saw the look on your face when you rediscovered them, and all those old memories came to the surface. You wouldn't have missed that for the world, and I wouldn't have either. Hearing your stories—"

When Anna abruptly stopped, Sylvia studied her over the rims of her glasses. "Don't stop there, dear."

Anna hesitated, but then she decided to confess the truth. "Hearing your stories makes me feel like I'm a real Elm Creek Quilter."

"You *are* a real Elm Creek Quilter," Sylvia exclaimed, astonished. "You became one the moment you agreed to join our staff."

"But you founding members have been through so much together. Sometimes I'm afraid I'll always be a newcomer, that I'll never find my place within your circle of quilters."

"Nonsense." Sylvia placed her hands on Anna's shoulders and looked her squarely in the eye. "You're one of us. Never doubt that. If my stories make you feel as if you belong, then I'll tell you stories until you feel as if you've experienced every celebration, every argument, every hard day's work, and every idle moment that passed within these gray stone walls. I'll tell you stories until you can't bear the sound of my voice any longer."

Anna couldn't help laughing. "You'd run out of stories before that happened."

"You'd be surprised, dear. Elm Creek Manor has a rich, storied history."

"I don't doubt that for a moment, or that we need to share that history with our campers so they feel it in every room of the manor." Anna turned slowly in place, studying the kitchen and considering the possibilities. The answer was there, nearby, if she could just put her finger on it. "Especially here. I've always believed that a kitchen should be the heart of the home. As the heart of Elm Creek Manor, this kitchen should preserve the past and present of the Bergstrom family and Elm Creek Quilts as no other place in the manor could."

"What do you suggest, dear?"

Anna's thoughts were racing so that she could barely keep up with them. "All those treasures we've discovered today, the family keepsakes that generations of Bergstroms have cherished. We need to display them here—just as we would at a Farewell Breakfast. It will be a continuous show-and-tell and sharing of memories so that everyone who enters this kitchen will know what a special place this is."

"But the tablecloth is half-ruined, and the aprons are worn almost threadbare." Suddenly Sylvia brightened. "But we don't need to save every scrap. We'll do as quilters have done since the dawn of patchwork."

All at once, Anna understood. "We'll salvage the usable pieces and sew them into a quilt."

Sylvia's eyes were bright with excitement as she strode to the bare wall near the hallway entrance and traced a large square in the air with her hands as if framing a work of art. "We'll display it here so our guests see it as soon as they cross the threshold. We'll sew blocks that tell the stories of all the special occasions and ordinary family meals we prepared in this kitchen. A Cut-Glass Dish block for my mother's favorite potluck serving piece, of course—"

"And a Harvest Home block, to remind us of the Harvest Dances the Bergstrom women prepared their best recipes for," Anna broke in. "Honeybee, for the quilting bees you hosted."

"And all the quilting bees we'll enjoy in the future," Sylvia agreed. "Fond Farewell, for the Farewell Breakfasts that wrap up each week of quilt camp. Friendship Square for National Quilting Day."

"Don't forget a Cornucopia block for your sister," Anna teased.

"I suppose we must." Sylvia gazed heavenward, feigning resignation. "The story of this quilter's kitchen wouldn't be complete without it. But I insist that our handiwork must surpass my sister's even if we must sacrifice historical accuracy for aesthetics."

"You make the quilt," said Anna. "I'll collect the recipes. Lucinda's cards are a wonderful beginning, but we have so many more to gather."

Just as they needed to preserve the precious scraps of heirloom fabric, so must they also preserve the wonderful flavors of Elm Creek Manor, past and present. Bergstrom family traditions and new camper favorites alike, because both, together, created the flavor of Elm Creek Quilts.

As evening fell and the tall trees on the banks of Elm Creek cast long shadows upon the manor, Anna and Sylvia felt their weariness lift, to be replaced by the sweetest anticipation.

They could only imagine what they would find within the quilter's kitchen the next day when they resumed their work—and the delicious flavors and exquisite quilt blocks their discoveries would inspire.

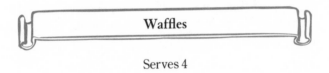

**Waffles**

Serves 4

¾ cup all-purpose flour

¼ cup cornstarch

½ teaspoon kosher salt

½ teaspoon baking powder

¼ teaspoon baking soda

¾ cup buttermilk

6 tablespoons canola oil

¼ cup whole milk

1 large egg, separated

1 tablespoon sugar

½ teaspoon vanilla extract

Place the flour, cornstarch, salt, baking powder, and baking soda in a large mixing bowl and combine well.

Place the buttermilk, oil, milk, and egg yolk in a small bowl and mix well.

Place the egg white in a medium bowl and whip using a whisk, to soft peaks, 2 to 3 minutes. Add the sugar and beat until firm. Add the vanilla extract.

Pour the liquid ingredients into the dry and whisk until just mixed. Gently add the egg-white mixture.

Pour into a waffle iron and proceed according to the manufacturer's directions.

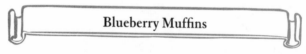

### Blueberry Muffins

Yield: 12 muffins

1¾ cups all-purpose flour

¼ cup cornmeal

⅔ cup sugar

2 teaspoons baking powder

½ teaspoon baking soda

½ teaspoon kosher salt

2 cups frozen blueberries

½ cup (1 stick) unsalted butter, melted and cooled

2 large eggs, at room temperature

1 cup plain low-fat yogurt or sour cream

2 teaspoons vanilla extract

1 teaspoon grated lemon zest

Preheat the oven to 375 degrees F. Line a 12-cup muffin pan with paper liners.

Place the flour, cornmeal, sugar, baking powder, baking soda, and salt in a small mixing bowl and mix well. Add the berries and gently toss until they are coated with the mixture.

Place the butter, eggs, yogurt, vanilla, and lemon zest in a large bowl and whisk well. Add the flour mixture by hand and stir until just combined. (Do not overmix.)

Fill each cup almost to the top. Transfer the muffin pan to the oven and bake until golden, 22 to 24 minutes. Cool 5 minutes, and then place on a wire rack to cool.

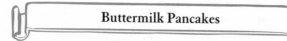

## Buttermilk Pancakes

Yield: twelve 6-inch pancakes

2 cups all-purpose flour
1 tablespoon sugar
1 teaspoon baking soda
2 teaspoons baking powder
½ teaspoon kosher salt
2 cups buttermilk
½ cup milk
2 large eggs
2 tablespoons unsalted butter, melted, or canola oil
Unsalted butter, for the pan
Pure maple syrup, for serving

Place the flour, sugar, baking soda, baking powder, and salt in a large bowl and stir to combine.

Place the buttermilk, milk, eggs, and melted butter in a small bowl and stir to combine. Add the wet ingredients to the dry ingredients and mix until just combined. Do not overmix.

Place a large skillet over medium heat and when it is hot, add the butter. Drop ladlefuls of batter on the surface of the skillet. Cook until bubbles form. Flip over and cook for about 2 minutes. Serve immediately with pure maple syrup.

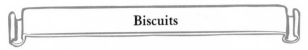

## Biscuits

Yield: 12 biscuits

1¾ cups all-purpose flour

1 tablespoon baking powder

1 tablespoon sugar

½ teaspoon kosher salt

4 tablespoons (¼ cup) unsalted butter, chilled and cut in slices

4 tablespoons (¼ cup) shortening, chilled and cut in pieces

½ cup heavy cream

Preheat the oven to 375 degrees F. Line a baking sheet with parchment paper.

Place the flour, baking powder, sugar, and salt in the bowl of a food processor fitted with a steel blade and mix to combine. While the processor is going, add the butter and shortening, a few slices at a time, and process until the mixture resembles cornmeal. Transfer the mixture to a large mixing bowl; add the cream and, using a wooden spoon, mix until combined.

Divide the mixture into 12 pieces, pat each down to ½ inch, and place them on the prepared baking sheet. Transfer to the oven and bake until golden brown, 12 to 15 minutes.

**Denver Omelet**

Serves 8

For the filling:

1 tablespoon unsalted butter

1 small onion, or 2 leeks, chopped

1 red bell pepper, diced

1 green bell pepper, diced

2 garlic cloves, minced

1 cup Virginia baked or smoked ham, diced

1 teaspoon kosher salt

For the omelet:

16 eggs, lightly beaten

¼ cup fresh Italian flat-leaf parsley,
    finely chopped

½ teaspoon Tabasco sauce

1 tablespoon butter

*To prepare the filling:* Place a 12-inch skillet over medium-high heat and when it is hot, add the butter. Add the onion, peppers, and garlic and cook until softened, about 10 minutes. Add the ham and salt and cook for 2 minutes. Transfer the mixture to a plate and set aside.

*To make the omelet:* Place the eggs, parsley, and Tabasco in a bowl and mix well. Reheat the skillet over medium-high heat and when it is hot, add the butter. When the butter has melted, add the egg mixture and gently swirl the pan until the eggs just begin to set. Add the filling and heat for 1 minute. Slide a large spatula under half the omelet and fold it over. Gently press down and remove the omelet from the skillet. Cut into eight slices and serve immediately.

### Glazed Ham Cooked in Beer and Brown Sugar

Serves 10 to 12

One 12- to 16-pound fully cooked Jones Ham,
     trimmed of as much fat as possible

For the glaze:

1½ cups dark brown sugar, loosely packed
1½ cups apricot preserves
½ cup Dijon mustard

Two 12-ounce bottles dark beer

Place the ham in a large stockpot, cover with cold water, and bring to a boil over high heat. Reduce the heat to low and cook for 1½ hours.

*Prepare the glaze:* While the ham is cooking, put all the ingredients in a small bowl and combine well (you can do this up to 1 week ahead of time).

Preheat the oven to 400 degrees F.

Transfer the ham, fat side up, to a cutting board, and using a very sharp knife, make a diamond pattern in the skin. Pack the glaze into the pattern's crevices and brush on the skin. Place it in a roasting pan big enough to fit the ham snugly. Pour the beer around the ham. Bake until the crust is deeply browned and crackly, about 45 minutes, basting every 10 minutes with the beer. If the beer evaporates, add water, about 1 cup at a time. Allow the ham to rest for 10 minutes before serving. Remove the glaze from the bottom of the pan and transfer to a small bowl. Serve with lots of different mustards and the glaze on the side.

## Apricots with Yogurt and Ginger Sauce

Serves 6

3 cups water

⅔ cup sugar

6 ounces dried apricots

Quarter-size piece of fresh gingerroot

Strips of peel from 1 lemon

⅓ to ½ cup whole-milk or Greek yogurt

Place the water, sugar, apricots, gingerroot, and lemon in a saucepan and bring to a boil over high heat. When the sugar has dissolved, about 3 minutes, reduce the heat to low and simmer until the apricots have plumped, about 30 minutes. Remove the apricots to a shallow bowl and return the pot to the stove. Boil until thickened, syrupy, and reduced by about half, about 8 minutes. Pour the syrup over the apricots, cover, and refrigerate at least 2 hours and up to 2 days. Discard the lemon strips before serving.

Serve the apricots with a dollop of yogurt and a drizzle of the ginger syrup.

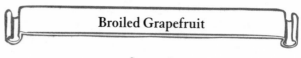

## Broiled Grapefruit

Serves 6

3 large grapefruits, halved
¼ cup light brown sugar
Mint leaves, for garnish

Preheat the broiler.

Place the grapefruits, cut side up, on a large baking sheet. Sprinkle with the brown sugar and transfer to the broiler. Broil until the top is browned and bubbling, about 5 minutes. Set aside for 3 to 4 minutes and serve, garnished with mint leaves.

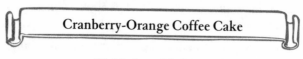

## Cranberry-Orange Coffee Cake

Yield: about 24 pieces

For the cake:

½ cup (1 stick) unsalted butter, at room temperature
1 cup sugar
2 large eggs

1 teaspoon vanilla extract

2 tablespoons orange juice concentrate

2 cups all-purpose flour

1 teaspoon baking powder

1 teaspoon baking soda

½ teaspoon kosher salt

1 cup sour cream

2½ cups fresh or frozen whole cranberries

For the topping:

¾ cup light brown sugar, loosely packed

½ cup all-purpose flour

2 teaspoons ground cinnamon

4 tablespoons unsalted butter, chilled and sliced

Grated zest of one orange

½ cup walnuts, coarsely chopped

Preheat the oven to 350 degrees F. Butter and lightly flour a 9 x 13-inch pan.

*To make the cake:* Place the butter and sugar in the bowl of a stand mixer fitted with a paddle and beat until creamy, 3 to 5 minutes. Scrape down the sides of the bowl, add the eggs one at a time, the vanilla, and the orange juice concentrate and beat after each addition.

Add the flour, baking powder, baking soda, and salt. Add

the sour cream and mix until smooth. Spread in the prepared pan and top with the cranberries.

*To make the topping:* Place the brown sugar, flour, and cinnamon in a small mixing bowl and toss to combine. Add the butter, in pieces, and mix until crumbly. Add the orange zest and walnuts and mix well. Sprinkle the topping over the cranberries.

Transfer to the oven and bake until a cake tester inserted in the center comes out clean, about 45 minutes. Serve warm or at room temperature.

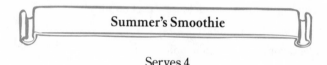

## Summer's Smoothie

Serves 4

2 overripe bananas, cut in 4 pieces each

1 cup fresh raspberries or blueberries

1 cup fresh strawberries

2 cups low-fat plain yogurt

1 cup orange juice

1 cup ice cubes

Place the bananas and berries in a blender or the bowl of a food processor fitted with a steel blade and process until almost smooth. Add the remaining ingredients and process until smooth. Serve immediately or refrigerate up to 1 hour.

# Metric Equivalents

OVEN TEMPERATURE EQUIVALENTS

| Description | °Fahrenheit | °Celsius |
| --- | --- | --- |
| Cool | 200 | 90 |
| Very slow | 250 | 120 |
| Slow | 300–325 | 150–160 |
| Moderately slow | 325–350 | 160–175 |
| Moderate | 350–375 | 175–190 |
| Moderately hot | 375–400 | 190–200 |
| Hot | 400–450 | 200–230 |
| Very hot | 450–500 | 230–260 |

# Acknowledgments

A special thank you to Sally Sampson who created the recipes for this book. Sally Sampson is the author or coauthor of numerous cookbooks, including the James Beard Award–nominated *The $50 Dinner Party*, *Throw Me A Bone* (with Cooper Gillespie), and *The Olives Table* (with Todd English). She has contributed to *Self, Bon Appétit, Food & Wine, The Boston Globe, Boston* magazine, and *The Boston Phoenix*. She lives with her family in Watertown, Massachusetts.

More of Sally's delicious recipes can be found in these fine cookbooks:

*Recipe of the Week: Ice Cream*

*Recipe of the Week: Burgers*

*Recipe of the Week: Cookies*

*Recipe of the Week: Kabobs*

*From Warehouse to Your House*

*Party Dips!*

*Souped Up!*

*Throw Me a Bone* (with Cooper Gillespie)

*Party Nuts!*
*The Occidental Tourist* (with Stan Frankenthaler)
*The Bake Sale Cookbook*
*The Olives Dessert Table* (with Todd English)
*The $50 Dinner Party*
*The Figs Table* (with Todd English)
*The Olives Table* (with Todd English)
*The Diet Workshop's Recipes for Healthy Living*
*Chic Simple Cooking*
*Recipes from the Night Kitchen*

# Recipe Index

**Cut Glass Dish**

**Corn and Beans**

**Honeybee**

**Broken Dishes**

**Churn Dash**

**Picnic Basket**